He turned her hand over and slowly undid the little buttons at the wrist of her glove, then drew off the glove and bent and kissed her wrist. His lips were warm. He then straightened up and looked into her eyes. Her face in the shadowy landing looked young and soft and her eyes enormous.

He placed both his long hands on either side of her face and bent and kissed her, his mouth now firm and hard, pressing down on her soft lips, which trembled under his own.

He sighed against her lips and wound his arms about her and lifted her up against his body. The rigid spasm of fear that had gripped her when he had first begun to kiss her, obscure, half-remembered memories of what men were supposed to do to women, ebbed away.

He released her lips and set her down and stood back a little, surveying her.

He put one long finger under her chin and tilted her face up, "Go to bed, Alice," he said quietly. "I' faith, you are very young."

Also by Marion Chesney
Published by Fawcett Books:

QUADRILLE
THE GHOST AND LADY ALICE
LADY LUCY'S LOVER
THE FLIRT
DAPHNE
THE FIRST REBELLION
SILKEN BONDS
THE LOVE MATCH
THE SCANDALOUS LADY WRIGHT
HIS LORDSHIP'S PLEASURE
HER GRACE'S PASSION
THE SCANDALOUS MARRIAGE
A MARRIAGE OF INCONVENIENCE
GOVERNESS OF DISTINCTION

THE
DESIRABLE
DUCHESS

Marion Chesney

FAWCETT CREST • NEW YORK

A Fawcett Crest Book
Published by Ballantine Books
Copyright © 1993 by Marion Chesney

All rights reserved under International and Pan-American Copyright Conventions. Published in the United States by Ballantine Books, a division of Random House, Inc., New York, and simultaneously in Canada by Random House of Canada Limited, Toronto.

Library of Congress Catalog Card Number: 92-97064

ISBN 0-449-22156-3

Manufactured in the United States of America

First Edition: March 1993

Chapter One

ALICE LACEY was the envy of her peers. She was the only child of rich and apparently doting parents, and she was, by the age of eighteen, already an acclaimed beauty—having glossy auburn hair, hazel eyes, and a perfect figure combined with a wide-eyed vulnerable look, a peculiarly untouched look, that somehow made all men long to possess her.

At her very first Season, she had fallen head over heels in love with Sir Gerald Warby, a handsome and charming man. Because her parents considered her too young, and because Sir Gerald did not command much of a fortune, there was as yet no formal engagement.

But Alice was content. Her parents would come about. Sir Gerald lived in the same county and was a constant visitor to Wold Park, her parents' stately home.

She would often stand on the belvedere outside the drawing room and look down the long drive for his arrival. She liked above all things to see him arriving on horseback like a knight of old. He was a fine figure of a man, with glossy black hair and black eyes. Her mother had pointed out that he was

1

a trifle long in the body and short in the leg, but Alice could see no fault in him.

She lived inside a glass bubble of happiness, young, confident, and very much in love. The death of the old Duke of Ferrant, whose estates marched with her parents', went by her sunny mind, casting only a slight shadow. The news of the arrival of the heir did not interest her.

Almost a year passed, and just before her nineteenth birthday—just before her parents were about to allow her permission to declare her engagement to Sir Gerald—the duke gave a ball at Clarendon, huge palace of the Dukes of Ferrant.

Alice gladly submitted to being dressed in her very best ball gown, for Sir Gerald was to be there . . . or so she thought. But before she was about to set out with her parents, his footman arrived with a message to say that Sir Gerald had fallen victim to the childhood illness of mumps.

Her happiness was dimmed, but she recovered her spirits by the time the Lacey carriage drove up to the magnificent entrance. A visit to Clarendon *was* an event. Her own home, gracious though it was, could not compete with the splendor of this great pile, this harmonious mixture of architecture old and new. The late duke had been something of a recluse and had never entertained, so this was the Laceys' first visit to the ducal home.

Her mother, Mrs. Lacey, had risen from the merchant class by marrying John Lacey, a member of the untitled aristocracy. She was an assured and well-dressed matron most of the time, but the magnificence of Clarendon, the sheer number and rich dress of so many liveried footmen, made her unusually flustered and self-conscious, and she gazed about her, her little rouged mouth slightly open in awe.

Alice had not yet met the duke. She had heard him described as handsome but had discounted this. In society, all dukes were handsome.

When she mounted the wide double staircase, he was waiting at the top to welcome his guests. He was an imposing figure of a man, quite old, probably thirty, which *was* old to Alice. He was very tall, with fair hair curled in the Windswept. His face was high-nosed and austere. His gray-blue eyes were long and looked surprisingly Oriental in such an English face. He had broad shoulders and a narrow waist and slim hips, but he looked like a cold, hard, domineering man, and, as his eyes searched her face, Alice blushed slightly and instinctively moved closer to her father for protection.

Most of the people in the ballroom were familiar to Alice as they all came from the county. She was surrounded immediately by her female friends, all chattering about this and that in a breathless way as their eyes slid past Alice to the doorway, where the duke was receiving the last of his guests.

"Will he dance with me, do you think?" asked Lucy Farringdon, a bouncy brunette with sausage curls. "Mama says one of us must catch him quick before turning him over to the competitions of the London Season. But you don't need to worry, Alice, you have your Sir Gerald."

"He looks quite a frightening gentleman," said Alice. "Ah, he has decided to join the guests in the ballroom."

The duke stood in the doorway, tall and remote in black coat and black evening breeches. Diamonds glittered in his cravat and on the buckles on his shoes. How very grand all the guests looked, thought Alice. Everyone had put on their very best clothes. Newly cleaned jewels, family heirlooms, winked and sparkled, sending prisms of light dancing across the polished floor. Where had old Lady Dunster found that enormous collar of diamonds and sapphires? And Mrs. Stables was wearing a heavy medieval necklace of huge stones, so badly cut that trapped light slumbered darkly in the depths of their unfaceted surfaces. All the ladies' waistlines followed the current fashion of being somewhere up under the armpits—even the genteelly poor Harris sisters—although one could easily see how, in their case, unfashionable dresses had been inexpertly altered for the occasion.

Alice, as befitted a debutante, was dressed in white muslin trimmed with priceless lace. She wore a simple necklace of coral and gold and a Juliet cap, all the rage, embroidered with bugle beads and rhinestones.

Lucy grabbed her arm and said, "He is walking toward us. The duke! Oh, I hope he asks me. I am sure Papa would double my pin money if only he would ask me."

Alice was aware that her parents had materialized at her side. She was aware of tension emanating from them.

The duke stopped and bowed. "My compliments..."

"Mr. and Mrs. Lacey," whispered a neat young man at his elbow.

"Ah, yes. Mr. and Mrs. Lacey. We are neighbors."

"My daughter," said Mr. Lacey, giving Alice a nudge in the back.

Alice curtsied, and the duke bowed.

"I would deem it a great honor, Miss Lacey," he said, "if you would have this dance with me."

Alice curtsied again. He held out his arm in a commanding way, and she placed the tips of her gloved fingers on it; he led her to the center of the floor, aware of the buzz and hum of gossip. The dance was the Sir Roger de Coverley, an energetic affair, and so, thought Alice with relief, gave little chance for conversation. It lasted half an hour. The duke danced well and gracefully, but Alice was all too aware of watching jealous eyes. She wished with all her heart Sir Gerald had not fallen ill. They would have gone in for supper together. They would have chatted easily. She would have felt at home with him, basking in the glittering admiration in his black eyes.

When the dance came to an end, she sank down in a curtsy. "You dance excellent well, Miss Lacey," said the duke. He held out his arm. Alice realized that, of course, she would have to promenade around the floor with him until the next dance was announced.

"I was not aware," he said, "that I had such a beautiful neighbor."

"You are too kind, Your Grace."

"But we must rectify that situation, must we not? I plan to entertain more."

"You will be extremely popular," said Alice. "Mostly we all wait until the London Season for our pleasures."

"Ah, you have had a Season? And still unwed? Are the gentlemen of London blind?"

Alice opened her mouth to tell him about Sir Gerald, but the voice of the majordomo sounded out, announcing the next dance.

"Alas, I must dance with someone else," he said. His odd eyes glinted down at her. "You must honor me again with the supper dance."

"Thank you, Your Grace," said Alice in a hollow voice.

Her hand was immediately claimed by another partner. She was very popular and, after the next dance was over, was immediately surrounded by a crowd of gentlemen competing to see which one she would favor with a dance. Alice laughed and teased and flirted—as any young lady was well trained to do—but then she heard her father's voice, asking her for a word in private.

He led her away from her courtiers to where her mother was standing. "My pet," said Mr. Lacey, "what did the duke say to you?"

"He paid me some pretty compliments," said Alice, "and asked me for the supper dance."

"Ah," said Mr. and Mrs. Lacey in unison, and exchanged glances.

"My love," said Mrs. Lacey, winding a maternal arm around her daughter's waist, "it is not the thing, you know, to tell a gentleman who takes you into supper, particularly your host, that you are in love with another. Not the thing at all. Very bad ton. We are sure you can be discreet."

"But he will know soon enough when the engagement is announced," exclaimed Alice.

"Of course, of course," said Mr. Lacey smoothly. "But you must be guided by us. We assure you it is not the thing. Think on't. What gentleman at his own ball, flattering a pretty young miss, wishes to hear of her affections for another?"

Alice's face cleared. "Of course, you are right. All this flirtation is such a hollow game, but I suppose

I had better mind my manners and play it or poor Sir Gerald will find his wife damned as an Original."

By the time the supper dance arrived, Alice felt calmer. She had noticed the duke seemed every bit as attentive to the other ladies he had danced with as he had been to her. When they had supper together, sitting at the head of a T shape of tables, he told her of his travels abroad and was amusing and informative. He asked no disturbingly personal questions, only easy ones of how she passed her days, and as Alice answered him, she realized for the first time that she led quite a busy life for a young lady of leisure. On Monday there was the club she had formed to make clothes for the poor; on Tuesday there was a round of the sick on her parents' estates; on Wednesday she read to the children at the parish school; Thursdays she set aside for making medicines in the still room; Fridays were given up to dancing lessons and French and Italian lessons; Saturdays to shopping and sewing and painting; and Sundays to church and rest. In the evenings, she would go out with her parents to visit friends or to some local Assembly.

He was friendly and attentive, and to Alice's naive eyes very much the polite older man listening to the prattling of a young girl. She forgot to be afraid of him, forgot about those jealous watching eyes—for what had they to be jealous of when her heart was Sir Gerald's?—and animation added a sparkle to her beauty. There was no question of more dances with the duke after supper. He had already danced with her twice. Three times would have been tantamount to a proposal of marriage.

Alice was too tired and happy on the road home

to notice that odd tension was still emanating from her parents. She was already composing in her mind the letter she would send to Gerald, telling him all about the ball.

The following day was a Saturday. Alice slept late, but she went to her writing desk as soon as she had washed and dressed, and wrote to Sir Gerald. She then ran downstairs and gave the letter to one of the footmen, asking him to take it to the stables and get a groom to ride over to Sir Gerald's with it.

Although she knew Sir Gerald would not call—the poor man was ill—she stood out on the belvedere through force of habit and was able to see the footman walking out across the lawns in the direction of the stables.

And then a voice hailed him. The footman stopped and looked back. Then he set off back to the house at a run. Alice waited impatiently for him to reappear. If he did not, then she would need to go downstairs, retrieve her precious letter, and send another footman with it.

Her mother's voice called to her from the door of the drawing room. "What are you doing, Alice?"

"I gave John the footman a letter to Sir Gerald to take over to the stables so that a groom might deliver it, but someone called him back," said Alice, turning round from the edge of the balustrade. "I hope he does not forget."

"I shall see to it, my pet," said her mother.

And so she had, thought Alice, as the footman soon reappeared and set off at a fast trot to the stables. She would have waited longer, waited to see the groom and horse disappearing down the drive, but the chill wind of autumn was tugging at her dress and ruffling her hair, so she went back inside, closing the long French windows behind her.

When she went down to the breakfast room, she found her mother and father in the hall, dressed to go out. "No need for you to come, my love," said her father. "We are just making a call."

"On whom?"

"Why, on old Mrs. Jones in the village," said Mrs. Lacey. "She is feeling poorly again."

Alice was surprised. Usually her parents did not trouble to visit the sick of the parish and often tried to stop Alice from doing so, saying the poor were notoriously infectious, just as if the rich never caught anything.

But Alice was content to let them go—for it meant she would be alone when Sir Gerald sent his reply. He always kept her servant waiting while he sent a letter of reply. But the long day wore on toward dusk and there was no sign of that precious letter. She swung a heavy cloak about her shoulders and walked over to the stables. She asked the head groom which servant had been sent to Sir Gerald's.

He bowed and said he had sent Sam.

"And is Sam not yet returned?" asked Alice.

"Returned this whiles back, Miss Alice."

"But that cannot be. He would have a letter for me."

"No, Miss Alice."

"I must ask him myself."

"Very good, Miss Alice," said the head groom. He sent a stable boy to fetch Sam.

Soon Sam appeared, a small, wizened man who looked like an old jockey.

"Now, Sam," said the head groom before Alice

could speak, "Miss Alice wants to know if Sir Gerald gave you a letter for her, which you know he did not, and you knows I expect you to be honest and not to be chattering away 'bout things what don't concern you. So—and your job stands or falls on it—you just answer yes or no to Miss Alice's question. Now, Miss Alice, you go ahead."

"Sam," pleaded Alice, "did Sir Gerald answer my letter? Did he give you a reply?"

"No, miss."

"You are sure?"

"Yes, miss." Sam's eyes flickered nervously to the head groom, who have him a slight nod of approval.

"Did you see Sir Gerald? Did you hand the letter to him personally?"

"No, miss. To a footman."

"And did the footman ask you to wait?"

Sam looked at the ground.

"Now, now, Miss Alice," said the head groom heartily. "You're making poor Sam's head spin with all these questions. He be a simple lad. Off you go, Sam."

There was nothing else for Alice to do but walk slowly back to the house. Her parents had returned. They were sitting before a roaring fire in the drawing room, drinking champagne.

"Come and warm yourself, my love," said Mrs. Lacey. "You look half-frozen."

"I went over to the stables," said Alice, holding her hands out to the blaze. "I was so sure Sir Gerald would have sent a reply to my letter. He must be very ill. Do you think, Papa, that we might drive over tomorrow just to see how he fares?"

"Actually, a letter did come for you by hand," said her father. "It is on the table in the hall."

Bright color rose in Alice's face and she darted from the room, ignoring her mother's cry of "Ladies do not *run*."

She seized the letter from the table in the hall, wondering why one of the servants had not brought it to her. But it was Gerald's writing and Gerald's seal.

She went up to her own private sitting room, clutching the letter to her breast.

She sat down by the fire and opened it.

At first she could not quite take in what the words said. It was incredible. Ridiculous! She began at the beginning and read it very slowly once more.

Dear Miss Lacey, she read, I am leaving to go on the Grand Tour and am still in an infectious state and so dare not call on you in person.

I shall be gone for some time and am writing to wish you all health and happiness. I do not expect you to wait for me. In fact, it was monstrous cruel of me to even dream of courting you when my intentions were none other than idle amusement and I was flattered that someone so young and beautiful as yourself should favor an old fellow like me.

Alice bit her lip. Sir Gerald was twenty-five.

Please forgive me, the letter went on, but I always was and always will be a sad rake.

Yr. Humble and Obedient Servant, G. Warby.

She threw the letter away from herself and burst into tears. She cried for quite some time and then, drying her eyes, picked up the letter again. Anger took over. How dare he! She had not imagined his protestations of love. It was he who had made all the plans of where they would live and what they would do when they were married.

A servant scratched at the door to say that supper was served and that her parents were waiting for her. She changed her dress and bathed her face and went downstairs to the dining room.

Her parents looked anxiously at her set face, but they said nothing until supper was served and the servants had withdrawn.

"What is up, Alice?" demanded her mother. "You look as if you have been crying."

"I have received a letter from Sir Gerald," said Alice in a thin voice. "He was only trifling with me. He has left to go on the Grand Tour."

"Monstrous," said her father, "but there was always something unstable and rackety about that young man. Better to find that out now than later. You are a great heiress, my dear, and must protect yourself from adventurers in future."

"But there was nothing in his manner to suggest anything other than that his affections were strongly engaged," cried Alice. "I am not a fool."

"You are a wise young lady most of the time," said Mrs. Lacey, "but men like Sir Gerald are experienced in the ways of deception. It would be best if you occupied yourself in the days to come and forgot about him completely. Believe me, his name will not be mentioned in this house again."

On Monday, as usual, Alice went down to the village of Lower Dibble to her sewing class of ladies who made clothes for the poor. She was accompanied by her lady's maid, Betty, a severe middle-aged woman who was efficient at her job but rarely spoke. The village hall, where the ladies met, was surrounded by elegant carriages.

Alice took a seat next to Lucy Farringdon, who was knitting rather than sewing. Lucy delighted in knitting stockings and scarves in a mixture of bright colors that delighted the peasantry they were meant for, most ladies considering the only suitable colors for the poor to be plain gray, and although Lucy was often chided on her extravagance in decking them out in bright reds and yellows, she refused to change, saying dull colors depressed her and it was depressing enough to be poor without being dingy as well.

"You were the success of the ball." Lucy sighed, her needles flashing. "Oh, if only the duke had even looked at me. And when he took you into supper, we were all nigh dying of envy. Not at all fair when you have your Sir Gerald."

"Not my Sir Gerald now," said Alice, taking a half-finished farm laborer's smock out of her workbag.

"Why? I heard he was ill. He is not seriously ill, is he?"

"Unfortunately, no," said Alice, stabbing her needle furiously into a hem. "He had the grace to write to me and tell me he had merely been trifling with my affections and is now gone on the Grand Tour."

"How dreadful!" Lucy gasped. "Are you heartbroken?"

"I do not know whether I am heartbroken or in a perpetual rage," said Alice. "I thought I was so lucky having indulgent parents who were prepared to let me marry for love."

"So now I suppose you are just like the rest of

us," said Lucy sympathetically. "I have my first Season next year, as you know, and it has been dinned into my head that I must be betrothed to anyone at all suitable by the end of it. Perhaps God should have made us poor," said Lucy, who believed like most of her peers that God put one in one's appointed station, "and then we could marry whom we pleased."

"I think romantic shepherds and shepherdesses exist only in poetry." Alice sighed. "Even the poor use their daughters as pawns to get a little more money. But Mama and Papa will not force me into marriage with anyone I do not like. I would rather not get married at all."

Lucy looked at her friend in alarm. "But the ignomy of being an old maid! Everyone sneers so. Then, unlike you, I have five little sisters who will all grow up and get married and I do not want to be the spinster aunt, passed from one household to another during my declining years. Besides, spinsters are odd, have you noticed?"

"I have often thought that spinsters might be happy enough were not society determined to find them odd," said Alice. "Please do something for me, Lucy. Only a few friends of mine—such as yourself—knew of my affection for Sir Gerald, for my parents would urge me not to talk about him until I was engaged." A tear ran down Alice's cheek and she brushed it angrily away. "Do not ever mention his name again."

"Gladly," said Lucy. "Although I would like to poison the man. But all saw him paying court to you. I shall say, if asked, that there was nothing to it."

Around them voices rose and fell, talking about

the duke, how handsome he was, how different life would be now that this new duke appeared determined to entertain.

"Will he come to your birthday party next week?" asked Annabelle Buxtable, a long-nosed young miss on Lucy's other side.

"My parents sent out the invitations," said Alice, "so I do not know whether he has been invited or not. It is not a very grand affair . . ."

Her voice trailed away and she angrily shook out the smock she was working on. She had dreamed about her birthday party. She had been so sure that she would have heard her engagement to Sir Gerald announced then. A special gown sent down from a famous London dressmaker's still lay in its folds of tissue. It was of the inevitable white muslin, but cut so cleverly with little puff sleeves, her first really low neckline, and with four flounces at the hem, with a spider gauze overdress fastening with silver clasps. How often she had imagined Gerald's black eyes when he saw her in that gown. Now he would not be there. There would be plenty of other young men from the county, but she was not interested in any of them—from the hunting-mad Lord Brent to the wispy and poetic Mr. Anderson, who claimed that his Scottish ancestry allowed him to actually see fairies dancing in the grass.

As she drove her little pony and trap back home, Betty, the maid, said suddenly, "I think I saw that duke riding off in the distance over the fields. I wonder whether he has been calling on Mr. and Mrs. Lacey."

"Perhaps," said Alice. "If he has, I am glad I have missed him. A very grand, formidable sort of man."

"Dukes always are," said Betty dismissively.

Alice found her parents in the downstairs Yellow Saloon, haranguing the servants. It transpired someone had left the door of the icehouse in the grounds open and the precious few blocks of ice, left over from the previous winter, had melted.

"Someone will need to go over to the Farringdons and beg some ice," said Mrs. Lacey, looking quite frantic. "What is a birthday party without ices? And all the furniture must be taken out of these downstairs saloons and stored. We must have decorations. Silk draped on the walls and hothouse flowers. An orchestra! We must have an orchestra."

"Mama, what is all this?" cried Alice. "We had agreed to have a few couples only; the drawing room would be enough for them with the carpet rolled back and the fiddler from the village."

"Fiddler from the— My stars, only hear the child! Alice, Ferrant is coming."

"But he will hardly expect us to compete with the grandeur of Clarendon," said Alice.

"We are not going to have the Duke of Ferrant damn us as shabby," said her father. "Leave all arrangements to us. He called here *in person* to pay his compliments to you, Alice. I did not tell him where you were, but he said he suddenly remembered your saying you sewed for the poor on Mondays. There was no need to tell him *that*."

All Alice could think in the days that followed was that she would be glad when her birthday was over. Another London Season was looming on her horizon. Her parents said they were opening up the town house again next year. Her heart ached for the fickle Sir Gerald.

She often stood on the belvedere, looking down the drive, hoping to see him ride up, hoping to hear him laugh and say it had all been a joke, that he still loved her and wanted to marry her.

But the day before her birthday party, she looked out and saw a gardener burning leaves over near the stables.

She went to the writing desk in her sitting room and took out a packet of letters that Gerald had sent her. Then putting on her cloak, she went down and out across the lawns to the bonfire.

She thrust the pile of letters into the blaze and then nodded to the under gardener, who stirred up the fire so that a tongue of flame from the letters shot up into the chilly autumn air.

Alice stood for a long time, her cloak wrapped tightly about her, gazing until all the letters had been reduced to ashes.

Then with dragging steps, she walked slowly back to the house.

Chapter Two

THE DUKE OF FERRANT took a clean cravat from his valet and applied himself to tying it in the Mathematical. His valet waited anxiously, more clean cravats at the ready, but the duke's deft fingers sculpted the starched muslin into place.

He was preparing to go out to Alice's birthday party. He had a gift already wrapped to take with him. It was a musical box, a pretty trifle made of carved sandalwood and lined with silk that played "My Heart's Desire," a song that had been popular for over ten years now. It was hard to know what to buy a young girl, as anything very expensive would be frowned on. He hoped he would not be the oldest there. What a vast gulf there seemed between his age and that of young Alice, a gulf caused not so much by years as by experience. He had fought in the Low Countries, in India, and then in the Peninsula before coming into the dukedom. Also Alice Lacey quite obviously had doting parents. He could barely remember his mother, who had died when he was six years old. His father had been a cold, austere man who had turned the training of his son over to servants to make sure he excelled in everything from riding, to shooting, to a thorough knowledge of the classics. It had been a lonely childhood. The only time he appeared to have pleased his father, the old duke, was when he expressed a desire to join the military at the age of sixteen. His father had bought him a commission in a crack regiment and had then apparently forgotten about his existence.

To the duke, a sensitive young man, the army was a brutal awakening. But he quickly adapted, and soon the end to his lonely life outweighed all other drawbacks. He never returned home on leave, preferring to spend his time in London before returning to the battlefront. He had never been in love but had enjoyed the favors and company of several experienced mistresses. He had never thought to marry but, somehow, now that he was a duke, now that he was settled and held the main position in the county and one of the highest positions in society, he found his thoughts frequently turning to marriage. He had gradually decided that the best prospect for a future wife would be a young girl who could be trained to the responsibilities of being a duchess. He thought about Alice Lacey. She was very beautiful and desirable; this evening, he would have an opportunity to study her further.

His butler entered and said, "Mr. Edward Vere has called, Your Grace."

The duke's face lit up. "Send him up immediately." Edward was his closest friend, but he had not seen him for over a year, for Edward had stayed with the regiment, right up to the surrender of Napoléon.

Edward Vere was a small, round, jolly man with a cherubic face and a mop of black curls that he desperately tried to tame into one of the fashionable styles without success. The duke hugged him and then stood back and gazed down at him affectionately. "Can you bear to get dressed very quickly and accompany me to a young lady's birthday party? Or are you too exhausted after your journey?"

"Fit for anything," said Edward, with a grin. "What's in the air? Marriage?"

"Only a social occasion. My neighbors, the Laceys, have an exquisite daughter. This is her nineteenth birthday."

"I should have a present for her. Can't go without a present."

"The family will understand. I shall send a footman on ahead of us to warn them of your arrival."

"Actually, I got something for you, but maybe it's more suitable for a lady."

"And what is that?"

"A parrot."

"Does it speak?"

"Not a word."

"Very suitable. Parrots are inclined to swear. It was a kind thought, but I would be delighted if you gave the bird to Miss Lacey. What is it called?"

"Polly."

"So original," mocked the duke. "Hurry and change. Take my man with you."

Soon both men set out, the bird in a cage between them. "That is not a parrot," said the duke, peering at it in the swaying light of the carriage lamp. "It's black. Parrots have gaudy colors."

"A sailor told me it was a rare black parrot," said Edward a trifle huffily.

"I saw something like that in a book," said the duke. "I have it! It's a *Gracula Religiosa*."

"Speak English."

"A mynah. Comes from Southeast Asia. Member of the starling family. I'm sure I read they were great talkers."

"Not this one."

"Have you been feeding it the right stuff?"

"I suppose so. Chap in the regiment said he knew of another chap who had one of these and told me what it ate. Eats like a horse, anyway."

"Its wings aren't clipped. Weren't you frightened it would fly away?"

"Haven't let it out the cage."

Edward sank back in his seat and closed his eyes. "Wake me up when we get there. I'm devilish tired and my corset is deuced uncomfortable."

"Why wear it?"

"Because," said Edward sleepily, "my evening coat is an example of Weston's best work and I couldn't get into it without my corset." Then he promptly fell asleep.

The duke surveyed him with affection. Edward's very presence was making thoughts of marriage fade away. The duke realized that a return to a certain amount of loneliness had started him thinking about marriage. The bird shifted awkwardly on its perch. "Poor thing," said the duke. "I shall make sure Miss Lacey buys you a very large cage so you can at least hop about."

Edward was slumbering so peacefully when they arrived at Wold Park, home of the Laceys, that the duke felt a pang of remorse at having to awaken him for what was surely going to turn out to be little more than a provincial children's party.

The house was blazing with light from top to bottom. The duke sighed. He hoped that the Laceys were as rich as he had heard them to be. In the short time since he had become a duke, he had been alarmed at the way mothers of hopeful daughters nearly bankrupted their husbands in their efforts to entertain him.

He woke Edward, and then both men entered the hall, a footman following, carrying the bird and the duke's gift.

The butler relieved them of their cloaks, and, taking their presents from the footman, the duke and Edward walked into the Yellow Saloon, where they had been told the guests were being received. Mr. and Mrs. Lacey stood at the entrance. The Yellow Saloon, the Green Saloon, and the Blue Saloon, all on the ground floor, had been opened up for the festivities. The walls were draped in swathes of silk and huge arrangements of hothouse flowers scented the air.

Alice Lacey was enthroned in a large chair at the end of the Yellow Saloon. She was surrounded with friends, and a table beside her was piled high with presents.

Edward thought she was the most beautiful creature he had ever seen. The low-cut white gown showed the excellence of her bosom. A small fairy-like diamond tiara was set amongst the burnished curls of her auburn hair and a thin string of diamonds was about her neck. Edward drew a deep breath. "Worth fighting for," he murmured. "That's the sort of lady I used to dream of on the battlefield, a true English rose."

Both men approached Alice, who stood up and curtsied. She shyly accepted the duke's gift and then exclaimed in surprise at the mynah. "How wonderful," she cried. "What is it called?"

"Polly," said Edward, pleased at the effect of his gift.

"Oh, that is too ordinary," said Alice. "What is it?"

"A mynah," said the duke. "A foreign bird. I would suggest it needs a larger cage."

The bird hunched on its perch and looked at Alice with bright, inquisitive eyes. "I am sure it is a he," Alice said, laughing. "I shall call him Oracle . . . because he looks so wise. What does he eat?"

"Loves fruit," said Edward.

Lucy Farringdon lifted a bunch of grapes from a bowl and gave it to Alice. "See if he will take one."

Alice held out a black grape, which the bird eyed inquisitively. She laughed with delight when Oracle seized it in his beak.

"He should talk, but he don't," said Edward.

"I am sure he shall." Alice summoned a footman and said, "Tell the smith I want a very large cage for this bird as soon as possible."

"What about my present?" said the duke. "Am I to be outclassed by Mr. Vere?"

She smiled at him and unwrapped his gift. She opened the lid. "My Heart's Desire" tinkled out. A shadow crossed Alice's face and she quickly snapped the lid shut. That had been their tune, hers and Gerald's.

"My present displeases you?" demanded the duke sharply.

Alice rallied. "No, Your Grace, it is vastly pretty . . . and so very kind of you to have brought it to me." She put it carefully on the table with the other gifts and turned her attention back to the mynah.

The duke and Edward bowed and walked off to talk to the other guests. But when they found themselves alone for a moment, the duke said, "My present seemed to give her pain."

"Nonsense," said Edward. "You're only huffy because she liked mine better."

And as the evening wore on, the duke thought he must have imagined that shadow on Alice's face. It was very much a country house party. They danced and performed charades while the fathers and mothers retired to another room and played cards. Alice sang for them in a light, pleasant if weak voice, and Lucy, who had become a great favorite with Edward, played the harp. Other young ladies performed, all vying with one another for the duke's attention. He tried not to watch Alice too openly, for he had to admit to himself that he found the girl captivating. By the end of the evening, he had made up his mind to marry her. She would make a beautiful duchess. She would inherit her parents' lands, which would in the future be added to his own, and the duke, like all aristocrats, was ever practical.

Alice laughed and talked and flirted, not too boldly, but in a well-trained way. Her fond parents looked on and smiled. Their party was a success. The ices were perfect, the orchestra good, and their honored guest was enjoying himself.

They had never quite got over having such a very beautiful daughter and so had assumed that anyone with such riches and beauty must be perpetually happy.

They did not guess, they could not guess, that after the party was over, when a red dawn was rising and the carriages of the guests were disappearing down the long drive, their daughter sat in her room, listening to the duke's music box, with tears of grief for her lost Gerald rolling down her face.

Alice began to guess her future in the following weeks. The duke was a constant caller. He was always courteous and correct, but there was a warmth growing in those normally cold eyes of his. One slight word from her would have stopped his attentions, but Alice, who felt she would never fall in love again, decided she might as well encourage the attentions of this duke and please her parents, who had done so much for her. Autumn moved into winter and there were sledging parties and skating parties, Christmas festivities, and more work for Alice to do among the poor to make sure they had enough to keep them warm.

Oracle, the mynah bird, was her only solace. She talked to it in the privacy of her room, where it hopped freely about its now huge cage. Little by little, she began to let it out, where it flew about the room and perched on the furniture and listened to her mourning for Gerald with bright, wise eyes until she could almost persuade herself that the bird understood what she was saying. But it did not speak. It either screeched or squawked or perched on her shoulder and leaned affectionately against her cheek making a crooning noise.

Spring spread slowly over the countryside, and bird cherry starred the hedgerows and daffodils grew on the lawns. When Alice went on a drive with the duke, it was usually in the company of others. Edward Vere was still staying with the duke and appeared to be becoming increasingly fond of Lucy. All the county seemed to accept the fact that Alice was the duke's intended bride.

But when her parents, dewy-eyed with pride, told her that the Duke of Ferrant had asked for her hand in marriage, it came as a cold shock. She begged for a little more time. Startled, they said that the duke was calling to see her that afternoon, that she had encouraged his affections, that she was being missish, and they looked so outraged at any suggestion that she should be other than over-the-moon with rapture and delight that Alice wearily gave in.

Betty, her maid, dressing Alice's hair for the great visit, broke into rare speech. "I have always thought," said Betty to Alice's reflection in the mirror, "that it is as well to draw back from something before it is too late. If you refused His Grace, there would be a great fuss and your parents would be very angry with you . . . and everyone would think you a fool. But time would pass and they would forgive and forget. It is your life and your future happiness you must think of."

"Thank you, Betty," said Alice wearily, "but I must go through with it. I will never love another man the way I loved Sir Gerald."

Betty twisted a curl delicately into place. "As to that, miss, did you ever really know Sir Gerald Warby?"

"What can you mean?"

"I mean that servants hear more than their masters or mistresses and I have heard some stories about Sir Gerald that might suggest he is not the gentleman he appeared to you."

"Enough, Betty. Never dare speak to me in such a manner again. I am only lucky to have had the love of such a fine man. He left because I was not worthy of him."

Betty relapsed into her usual taciturn silence.

Alice walked slowly down the stairs, feeling as cold and lifeless as a well-dressed doll. She was wearing a gown of pale blue jaconet muslin made with a gored bodice and finished with a tucker of fine embroidery. The weather was still chilly, and so she wore a Norfolk shawl around her shoulders— a shawl that her mother plucked away with an exclamation of impatience outside the drawing room, saying with a hiss, "He has ten minutes to make his declaration. Act prettily, miss."

The duke was standing by the fireplace when she walked in.

She stood before him like an obedient child.

"Do you know why I am come?" he asked gently.

"Yes, Your Grace."

"And will you do me the inestimable honor of agreeing to become my wife?"

A short silence. Then she said again, "Yes, Your Grace," in a flat voice.

He had to confess he was disappointed. He had begun to desire her more and more as the days had passed. But she was a young virgin, he reminded himself sternly. So he drew her to him and planted a kiss on her cold forehead. "There is no reason to be afraid of me," he said. "I am not going to press any intimacies on you at this stage. We will get to know each other a great deal better in the days leading up to our wedding in the summer."

Her eyes flew to meet his. "The summer! S-so soon?"

"Your parents have informed me that in view of this forthcoming marriage there is no need for you to attend the London Season. Nor is there any need to delay the wedding beyond this summer, is there?"

"Oh, no, not at all, Your Grace," said Alice, with dreadful politeness.

"This will not do, Alice," he said, with a quick frown. "We had come to be easy in each other's company. Let us return to our usual friendship. How is Oracle? Has he pronounced yet?"

"He is a very silent bird," said Alice, somehow relieved that the marriage discussion was over—so that she could pretend it had never happened. "I talk to him daily, and he seems to understand what I am saying."

"Clever bird. Now I know the interests of the poor of the parish are close to your heart and so I wanted to discuss improvements to the almshouses with you."

He talked on, and by the time Alice's parents entered the room, the couple were sitting side by side on the sofa, chatting amiably.

All Alice's fears rushed back as her parents congratulated them both. The duke took his leave, and Mrs. Lacey immediately began to discuss plans for the wedding.

Somehow Alice could not even voice her doubts and worries to her friend, Lucy. Lucy was in love with Edward Vere, the duke was Edward's friend, and therefore the duke must be all that was good and kind.

Then all the wedding arrangements took over and Alice had to be pinned and fitted for her trousseau. The sunny days flew past, quicker and quicker, like a speeding mail coach, until Alice decided she must never think of Gerald again.

On the evening of her wedding, Alice said mournfully to her mynah bird, "I must say good-bye to Gerald and never, ever think of him again. But I shall never love any man more." The bird squawked and hopped to the floor in front of her, its head on one side.

"But you shall come to the wedding breakfast," said Alice, "and everyone will spoil you and feed you lots of grapes. You will have a place of honor behind my chair."

Betty appeared and silently started to get her young mistress ready for bed.

When Alice was finally climbing into the high bed and the maid had retired, she suddenly heard the sound of a horse's hooves thudding up the drive. She ran to the window and looked out, but all was in darkness, and there was no balcony or belvedere outside her bedroom window to stand on and look over. That was the way Sir Gerald used to ride up to the front door, hell-for-leather. From below came the sounds of a bitter and noisy altercation. She opened the window. Her father's voice rose sharp and angry and edged with fear, "Get you gone. And if you come here again I shall shoot you."

With a gasp, Alice seized a wrapper, swung it around her, and ran downstairs. As she reached the hall, the great main doors were being locked and bolted by two of the footmen. Her mother stood there in her dressing gown, holding a candle, ashenfaced.

"Who is it? What happened?" cried Alice.

All looked up at her, all still as if frozen to the spot, her father, his fists clenched, her mother's face blanched, the footmen, and the butler.

Then her father moved forward. "Go to bed, my

dear. Nothing for you to worry about. Some wild Irishman who thought his doxy was a servant here. I sent him about his business."

Mrs. Lacey quite visibly rallied. "Such uncouth men frighten me," she murmured. "Come, Alice."

Alice allowed herself to be led back upstairs. When she had heard the sound of those horse's hooves, for one glorious moment she had thought it was Gerald riding back to her.

But before she went to bed, she reminded herself fiercely that Gerald had rejected her, had written that awful letter to her. To dream about seeing him again was silly and childish.

The morning was taken up with the long, laborious process of dressing. Her gown was of white silk embroidered with silver thread and seed pearls; her headdress of pearls and gold and real white roses. A hairdresser had been brought down from London to arrange her hair.

I am going to be married. I am going to be a duchess, she thought over and over again, but none of it seemed real. She could not think of the duke as a real person; she saw him more as an authority figure, more as someone who had commanded her to marry him—although he had not—like a royal command, rather than a request, and she buried deep in her heart the guilty thought that if she had refused him, he would have accepted that refusal without protest. Now it was too late to turn the clock back. What had they talked about? Well, they had talked about books, about agriculture, about wildflowers, about plays, about working for the poor, about a multitude of subjects . . . and yet never about their real feelings.

The wedding service was to be held in the village church of St. Paul's, with the wedding breakfast afterward in her home, Wold Park. As she sat by the window in her sitting room, stiff and regal in her finery, maids scurried about packing up all her belongings into large trunks for removal to the duke's home.

The relatives on Alice's side would all be her father's. She had never seen any of her mother's sisters or brothers. Mrs. Lacey had ruthlessly cut herself off from the merchant class. But she might have relented and asked a few of the more presentable ones to the wedding had not her daughter been marrying a duke. Mrs. Lacey sparkled with pride and happiness.

The time came for Alice to go downstairs and, with her father, travel in a flower-bedecked carriage to the church. It was a perfect summer's day, heavy with the scent of roses. All the tenants, in their finery, waited outside to give Alice a cheer and then follow the carriage on foot. Some threw flowers into the carriage. Alice wished veils were still fashionable, for she found it a great strain to smile and look happy.

From the minute she arrived at the dark little church, it all seemed like a dream.

She gave all her well-rehearsed responses, barely looking at the duke, although conscious of the finery of his white silk wedding coat. Lucy, in blue muslin and pink roses, was bridesmaid, and Edward Vere was bridesman.

And then it was over. The bells in the old steeple rang out over the countryside.

Alice emerged, blinking in the sunlight, on the arm of her husband. Her husband! She stole a look up at his face. He looked much younger and very happy. She took her place in the carriage, bewildered by the noise of the bells and the cheering of the villagers and tenants, by the rain of rose petals and small bouquets. One little bouquet of pink roses landed in her lap. She saw there was a note attached to it, a little spill of paper. She stole a look at the duke. He was smiling and waving to the crowds. She opened the little piece of paper and looked down. The few words made her gasp. "Meet me in the rose garden at two, Gerald."

She crushed the note in her fingers and stared around her at the crowds, looking for that beloved familiar face but not finding it. Why had he written to her, this day of all days, just when she was married to another?

She looked back at the church clock. Noon. She would need to make some excuse to slip away from the festivities.

Long tables were spread about the lawns so that all the villagers and tenants could share the wedding feast.

Inside, the duke led his new bride to the top table. Behind Alice, Oracle peered brightly from a gilt cage decorated on top with a white bow.

During the wedding breakfast, Alice smiled automatically and ate and drank little, her eyes always straying to a clock on the mantelpiece at the other end of the room. At five minutes to two, she murmured to the duke, "Excuse me for a moment."

"Don't be long, my love," he said. "The speeches are about to begin."

Alice left the room quickly and passed through the chain of saloons to a small morning room at the end that had French windows opening onto a terrace. From there, she could descend to the rose garden.

The rose garden was walled and screened from the lawns at the front of the house, where the villagers and tenants were celebrating.

She ran down the mossy steps, feeling herself enclosed by the warmth of the sun and the scent of the tumbling cascades of red and white roses.

And there, by a sundial in the center of the garden, stood Gerald. He was dressed in a suit of black velvet. His face was tanned. He looked older, grimmer.

"Gerald," whispered Alice.

He caught her in his arms and held her close. "Why did you leave me?" pleaded Alice.

"Your parents forced me," he said huskily. "They called on me that day I got your last letter. They said they would never allow me to marry you. They said I had to write a letter to you breaking off our relationship. Your mother cried. I thought I was doing the right thing. But when I heard you were getting married, I thought my heart would break."

"Oh, Gerald," said Alice, her voice breaking on a sob, "let us run away together. The duke will have the marriage annulled and then we can be happy."

He pressed her face against his chest so that she should not see the sudden calculation in his eyes. Mr. Lacey had paid him a vast sum to take himself off, but he had run through it, traveling and gambling and wenching to his heart's content. If he took Alice away, they would surely pay to have her back.

Children, bored with the festivities, had been feeding Oracle grapes soaked in brandy. In front and below the bird sat the Duke of Ferrant, who was watching the entrance to the long dining room, wondering whether he should send someone to find out what had happened to his bride.

"Howd'ye do?" squawked the mynah suddenly.

"It speaks! It speaks!" cried the children.

The guests fell silent, all looking at the bird and waiting for it to say something again. Oracle let out a raucous cry.

"Perhaps that's all it can say," said the duke, getting to his feet.

"Make it say something else," pleaded one of Lucy Farringdon's little sisters.

The duke smiled. "Speak, Oracle. I command you."

The bird put its head to one side. "Gerald," it rasped. "*Squawk.* Say good-bye to Gerald. Good-bye to Gerald. *Squawk.* Never love any man more. Gerald," and the bird finished its repertoire with a deafening whistle.

The duke noticed that Mrs. Lacey had turned a muddy color, that Lucy was looking frightened, and that after a shocked silence the guests had all begun to talk again in loud voices.

He went quickly from the room. Two footmen were on duty in the hall.

"My wife?" he demanded.

"Her Grace went through that way," said one of the footmen and pointed down through the chain of saloons. The duke walked quickly along. All the doors were open. He came to the little morning room and noticed the French windows standing open. He stepped out onto the terrace.

His wife, his new bride, was being held in the arms of a man . . . and the man was bending his head, about to kiss her.

The duke strode down to the garden and seized Gerald by the collar, then punched him with all his force on the chin; Gerald dropped like a stone and lay among the roses.

"You've killed him!" screamed Alice.

"Not yet, but I will," he said, ice-cold with anger. "Who is your lover?"

The enormity of what she had done to him, to this husband of hers, flooded over Alice.

"We were friends," she said. "We were to be married, but my parents forced him to go away, to write me a letter that it was all over. He came to say good-bye," she lied, for she now felt if she told the truth—that she had been on the point of running away with Gerald—he would kill him.

"And you have been pining for him, and sighing for him, and driveling over him this age. Yes, your damn bird decided to talk in front of the wedding guests. You had only to tell me ... to give some sign ... We will talk of this later. You will come back to the wedding breakfast—and you will smile and smile and say not a word of this. Do you understand? We will talk of this when we are in private."

"But Sir Gerald ..."

"He will recover and take himself off. Come, you wanton baggage."

He took her arm and marched her back indoors. Before they reached the hall, he released her. "Now find somewhere in your selfish heart a thought for everyone at this wedding and play the part of a happy bride—or I will shame you in front of your friends and parents."

Numbly Alice entered at his side. "I thought she had escaped me," cried the duke. He seized Alice in his arms and kissed her warmly on the mouth to cheers from the guests. He led her back to her seat. He flicked a glance at the mynah. "Remove the bird," he ordered a footman. "It has become too noisy."

The rest of the meal was a nightmare for Alice. Speech followed speech, toast followed toast.

Edward Vere sat studying the duke's face with worried eyes. He had asked Lucy about this Gerald the bird had been talking about, and Lucy had told him about Sir Gerald Warby. Edward had been shocked and had said roundly that the morals of young girls these days was disgraceful. Lucy, near to tears, now sat silently next to him.

At last the duke led his bride out. More rose petals, more cheers. The carriage moved off, children running alongside, a glimpse of Mrs. Lacey's face, white and tense. The couple smiled and waved all the way to Clarendon. The shadow of the great pile seemed to swallow them up. All the duke's servants were still at the festivities.

He led her into the library. "Sit down," he said. "We have been married in the sight of God and must make the best of this farce. Are you still a virgin?"

"Your Grace!"

"Enough of your missish airs. I repeat: Are you a virgin?"

"Of course," said Alice, white to the lips. He stared at her coldly. "I believe you. You may remain so until you are twenty-one, by which time I shall expect you to present me with an heir. You will not take lovers. I do not want my inheritance to go to a bastard. If I take mistresses, then you have only yourself to blame. You will not confide in anyone. You will be my duchess and will run my household. You have already been shown your rooms. Go to them and try to keep out of my sight as much as possible."

"Release me from this marriage," begged Alice.

"You have not even begun to suffer enough to repay me for the humiliation and hurt inflicted on me this day," said the duke. "Get you hence."

"What of Oracle? Have you killed the bird?"

"Why? Why take my spite out on a bird that was merely repeating the maudlin sighings of its mistress? Ah, but come with me; there is something I wish to get rid of."

They walked up the grand staircase, a stately couple in their wedding finery. "These, as you know, are your apartments," said the duke. "Ah . . . here we are."

He walked to a table and picked up the music box he had given her and flicked up the lid. The tinny, sentimental music filled the room. He walked to the open window and hurled it out.

"I do not care what you do with your life as long as you remain chaste," he said, swinging round. "Oh, God, to think I have wedded a silly, heartless, empty-headed, vulgar little slut!"

Alice sat down slowly after he had left, staring around the ornate magnificence of her new quarters, hearing the distant sounds of merriment. She tried to think about Gerald, to worry about Gerald, but the shame of what she had done to the duke finally engulfed all other thoughts.

Chapter Three

£ONDON. Almost a year had passed since Alice's wedding to the duke. They had taken up residence in the duke's town house, a massive building where she could as easily lose herself from the duke's sight as she could in the country.

One consolation for Alice was that Lucy, recently married to Edward Vere, was also in London and a constant caller. Alice felt she had shamed the duke enough over her behavior at the wedding and so had confided in no one about the miserable state of her marriage. The servants must have known something was badly wrong, that silent army who came and went during the day, ever courteous, ever watchful. She had been able to take up the reins of control easily. Before her marriage, she had been highly respected by the duke's servants because of her charitable work, and so there was no autocratic housekeeper or pompous butler to cope with. Her commands were always obeyed. She sometimes wondered if she could have made a life for herself on the stage, she acted the part of happy wife so well. Apart from Lucy, she had a small circle of friends among the other young society matrons, and, as their husbands were often absent at their clubs or at the House of Lords, they saw nothing odd in Alice's solitary existence. The duke and Alice often appeared together at balls and parties in the evening, and because society considered it very odd for a man to dance with his own wife, it was not considered strange that the couple should barely exchange a word, and only the duke's servants knew that the duchess often returned alone when the evening was over, the duke going off to either his club or some other place.

But even that little show of intimacy disappeared when the duke informed Alice, through his secretary, that he considered it a better idea if they shared out the many invitations: he would accept some and she the other. And that was when the cracks in the marriage began to show in public.

Lucy, attending a ball at the home of Lord and Lady Baxham, a ball to which she had not intended to go, only changing her mind at the last minute, was surprised to see the duke arriving with a mature beauty on his arm. She asked questions and found that the beauty was a certain Lady Macdonald. Lord Macdonald had died some time ago. Lady Macdonald was a voluptuous redhead with wide blue eyes and a style of dress that just bordered on the indecent.

"Does Alice know of this?" Lucy asked fretfully on the road home.

"No need for her to know," said Edward awkwardly. "I mean, such things go on. Vulgar to talk about 'em."

Lucy's eyes were wide and dark with anxiety. "But Edward, surely *you* have not . . . would not . . . ?"

He laughed and gave her a quick kiss. "Don't be silly, puss. Of course not."

"Then why . . . ?"

"Leave it alone, my precious."

"But it is all so odd. I was visiting Lucy t'other day and the duke came into the drawing room. He bowed, Alice curtsied, and then he went out again. They never exchanged a word. It's something to do with that wretched bird of hers, I know it! When it started talking at the wedding, I could have screamed."

"Yes, I thought he would have shot that bird. I wish I'd never brought it. Has it said anything since?"

"Only things like 'Good day, ladies' and 'Grapes, please.' He is a great favorite with children. Alice adores Oracle."

"Humph. Well, I would not worry, Lucy. Alice is a duchess and lives in such vast palaces of places that she can live a separate life in comfort."

"But she must be so unhappy. I should be devastated if you never spoke to me, Edward. Do try to find out from Ferrant what is going on with this Lady Macdonald."

"Hey, I can't go about asking a fellow about his mistress!"

"Then she is . . . Oh, *Edward.*"

"Now, then, why don't you have a word with Alice? Probably find she knows all about it and turns a blind eye."

But Lucy, calling on Alice the next day while her husband went off to a prizefight in the country, found Alice entertaining a group of matrons and had no opportunity to ask her anything.

One of Alice's guests, however, was different from the usual society lady, being an Irish colonel's wife, a Mrs. Duggan. She was plainly dressed and plain-spoken, and Lucy had found herself gravitating to her matronly warmth. Feeling in need of an ally, she shyly suggested that Mrs. Duggan might care to return to her home with her for tea, and the Irishwoman placidly accepted.

After Lucy had chattered nervously over the tea-cups of this and that, Mrs. Duggan at last interrupted her by saying, "Why not tell me what is on your mind, m'dear?"

Lucy started nervously and then gave a shame-faced laugh. "Is it so obvious? I am concerned about Alice, Duchess of Ferrant."

Mrs. Duggan nodded her head so that the huge plumes on her hat bobbed and shook. Her round apple face, with its small periwinkle eyes, creased in folds of sympathy. "Lady Macdonald," she said.

"Ah, yes." Lucy leaned forward. "Why does Ferrant squire her so openly?"

"Sure, she's his mistress—or so folks are saying."

"Oh, Mrs. Duggan! Surely not."

"Can't blame the duke, now can you?"

"Of course I blame him," said Lucy, amazed. "Who would not?"

"Well, now, I'm an old gossip, but there is a nasty little story running about—about how our duchess was secretly in love with one Sir Gerald Warby, so much so that she confided her feelings to that clever talking bird and the bird talked right at the couple's wedding."

"I'll strangle that bird," said Lucy miserably.

"And what good would that be doing? The damage is done. Although I sometimes wonder if Ferrant knows what he is doing. Lady Macdonald may look like a trollop, but she's a member of society

41

. . . and it is my belief she has ambitions to become a duchess."

"He would never get a divorce!"

"Such things have been known. It could be he could get an annulment. Our duchess has a virginal and untouched look, and there's no sign of an heir."

Lucy covered her face with her hands. "If only I could help her."

"There now," said Mrs. Duggan. "You musn't distress yourself. Bad for the baby."

"How did you know?"

"I can tell. Now I am going to Mrs. Fairchild's musicale tonight. I'll see what I can do."

Alice was walking through the vast echoing tiled hall of her husband's town house that evening followed by her maid. She was dressed to go out to the musicale. Before she reached the front door, held open for her by two footmen, the library door opened and her husband stood there looking at her.

She curtsied formally. He studied her for a moment as if taking in all the glory of embroidered white silk and the sparkle of the Ferrant diamonds—and then he retreated into the library and quietly closed the door.

She felt a lump rise in her throat and blinked away threatening tears.

A vision of Lady Macdonald, that cool, amused redhead, rose before her eyes to haunt her. Mrs. Harry Simms, a gossipy rattle of a matron, had pointed her out to Alice in the Park and had said, "You must feel like killing her." Pressed by the astonished Alice for reasons why she would want to kill a lady she did not even know, Mrs. Simms, after a great pretense of reluctance, gleefully divulged that Lady Macdonald and the Duke of Ferrant had been seen out together on many occasions.

Sometimes Alice had thought of begging her husband for a divorce to free her from the weight of guilt. The fact that she had shamed him at the wedding burned deeper into her soul each day. The mynah never mentioned Gerald's name these days. It had done so a few times but had quickly found that Gerald's name meant no fresh fruit. Alice did not know of the gossip about her disastrous wedding that was beginning to circulate. One disappointed mother of a hopeful daughter had told her best friend "in confidence," and the little ripples of gossip had spread out from this stone and had finally washed up in London. Now her husband was reportedly in love with another woman and must long to be free.

As soon as Alice walked into that musicale, she sensed something in the overheated air. Eyes glanced at her covertly, voices were lowered, people whispered. She was glad to see the bulk of Mrs. Duggan heaving up in her direction.

"You must be the most beautiful woman in London," said Mrs. Duggan in a bracing way. "We shall sit together and you shall tell me all the gossip."

Mrs. Duggan piloted Alice to a couple of chairs at the side of the music room. "I do not know any gossip," said Alice, "or rather, I hear a lot of it, but it goes in one ear and out of the other."

"Would to God that the rest of society was the same," said the Irishwoman piously.

Alice looked around. Society was chattering away: men were waving lace handkerchiefs and snapping open and shut snuffboxes; women were waving fans, the older ones flirting automatically, although their days of attracting any man were considered by the cruel to be long over. She leaned forward. "Tell me about Lady Macdonald."

Mrs. Duggan let out a little sigh. "So you know about that. It was bound to happen."

"Why?"

"The gossips have it that you humiliated your husband on your wedding day. The Oracle gave forth and named Sir Gerald Warby as your love."

"I shall never live that down. Never!" said Alice bitterly. "I barely see my husband now. We never talk. And it is the waiting and waiting. We cannot go on like this. Why does he not divorce me?"

"Divorce is extremely rare and a scandalous process. The print shops would have a high old time. Perhaps your husband loves you."

Alice gave a shudder. "He loathes me. There is worse, you see. Sir Gerald sent me a note on the day of my wedding, asking me to meet him in the rose garden of my home. He told me he had spurned me because my parents had told him to do so. I—I wanted to run away with him. Then Ferrant came on the scene and knocked poor Gerald out cold."

"Is that all? Sure, 'tis a mercy he did not kill him."

Alice said in a low voice, "I sometimes feel the weight of guilt too hard to bear."

"Do you love your husband?"

"No, but I bitterly regret my behavior. We are married in the sight of God."

"*Tish!* How grim and serious. If you want your husband to care for you enough to cease seeing this Lady Macdonald, then I suggest you begin to cast off your guilt and enjoy yourself. Your very fear and cringing must make him loathe you the more. *He* is not crawling about, head bowed with shame, because of his liaison with Lady Macdonald, now, is he, m' dear? You are young, and the young are allowed to make mistakes. Lady Macdonald is a full-blown beauty. But you are young and fresh."

Alice took a slow breath. "I have deliberately avoided going to the same functions as my husband, first because it was his idea and then because I did not want to see him enter the room with Lady Macdonald on his arm."

"Then go into battle! If you feel you owe him something, then get him out of the clutches of Lady Macdonald. She is greedy and avaricious—and 'tis said she drove poor old Lord Macdonald into his grave."

"Mrs. Duggan, I do not know how to thank you. I have had no one to turn to for advice. Mrs. Vere is too young and happy to be burdened with my problems. I have been estranged from my parents because I felt they had betrayed me. I know Sir Gerald would not have rejected me had they not interfered."

"As to that," said Mrs. Duggan cautiously, "has it ever dawned on you that had the roles been reversed, *you* would never have given up Sir Gerald without a fight?"

"Who knows what they really said to him," replied Alice impatiently. "They probably told him I loved Ferrant."

"Did Sir Gerald tell you that?"

"No, but—"

"Shhh. The music is about to begin." Mrs. Duggan sat back in her chair, well satisfied. She decided she would not pursue the subject of Sir Gerald

Warby, because any criticism of the man might only make Alice stubbornly keep him up on a pedestal.

She closed her eyes and thought instead of her husband, who was stationed in Paris. She would join him in two months' time, and in that two months, she meant to see if she could make this pretty duchess happy. She had faithfully followed her husband through the rigorous campaigns of the Peninsula, only this year leaving his side to travel to London to see the birth of her first grandchild. Now her daughter and baby were doing well, she could turn her attention to Alice. Strategy, that was what Alice needed. Just like in a military campaign. Mrs. Duggan fell asleep and began to snore gently in a sort of counterpoint to the music.

Alice received a visit from Mrs. Duggan the following afternoon. "I am come," said the Irishwoman, "to see if you plan to attend the Sandwells' ball."

"I planned to go to the opera this evening with Lucy Vere and Edward," said Alice. "The Sandwells' ball is to be attended by my husband and so— Oh, I see."

"Exactly, my love. Into battle. Send a note round to Mrs. Vere and cancel the opera. The Sandwells' ball it is. You will be chaperoned by me."

"He might be angry," said Alice cautiously. "Oh, and I have already told Lady Sandwell that I would not attend."

"And I told her you had made a mistake and that you would attend," said Mrs. Duggan. "Have you anything dazzling to wear?"

"I had an enormous trousseau made and have worn some of the gowns only twice."

"Listen to the chit!" Mrs. Duggan raised her

pudgy hands in exasperation. "You are married to one of the richest men in England. You must start ordering the finest gowns. And this drawing room? What d'ye think of it?"

Alice looked about her. It had heavy Jacobean furniture and heavy plum-colored curtains at the windows. A huge oil painting of a stag being savaged by hounds hung over the fireplace.

"In truth, I do not like it very much," she confessed.

"Then change it! Make your stamp on the duke's household. The drawing room is always the ladies' room."

"I would need to ask his permission."

"As to that, he'll give it readily, because at the moment he don't think he cares what you do."

Alice's face lit up in a rare smile. "Mrs. Duggan, I fear you are a disruptive influence."

"Isn't that after what Colonel Duggan is always saying! But he always has to admit, my interfering in things always works out for the best. Now let's go up and look at that wardrobe of yours."

A few moments later, Mrs. Duggan was shaking her head over the array of white muslin, silk, and satin ball gowns. "All very *jeune fille*," she mourned. "You need color, and we have hardly any time at all, at all. Now just let me send one of your servants round to Madame Duval and we'll have her round here like a shot."

Despite her wealthy upbringing, Alice had had stern rules of economy dinned into her head by her parents and governess. It seemed profligate in the extreme to send for London's leading dressmaker when she already had so many gowns to wear. But Mrs. Duggan had her way. Madame Duval mourned the lack of time, but servants were sent running between her workroom and the duke's house. Mrs. Duggan left them all to it and went off to her own home to change for the ball, returning in time to see a new duchess, one with large sparkling eyes, wearing a slip of white satin worn under an over-dress of French gauze painted with Chinese roses. Ropes of pearls had been twisted into the burnished curls of her auburn hair by the court hairdresser, who had also been summoned by Mrs. Duggan before she had left to go and change her own gown. The gauze overdress floated gracefully about the duchess's perfect figure and the lowered neckline of the gown exposed the top halves of two excellent breasts.

"I feel very daring . . . half-naked," said Alice, with a rueful laugh.

"You are fully armed for the battle," said Mrs. Duggan, herself resplendent in plum-colored satin.

"I heard Ferrant leave half an hour ago," said Alice. "We are a trifle late."

"And isn't that the idea, child? We shall make an entrance."

The Duke of Ferrant stood talking to a group of friends, Lady Macdonald on his arm. Contrary to the belief of society, he had not yet shared her bed—but he had more or less made up his mind to accompany her home that very night. She was very attractive, with a seductive, husky laugh. Her perfume was alluring, and he was conscious of the beauty of her breasts, exposed in a way that he would not have allowed in his wife. His wife! That caused a shadow to cross his face. The time was fast approaching when he would need to make up his mind about his marriage. Brief glimpses of Alice looking hangdog and miserable only increased his distaste for the whole sorry farce. Let her go and be happy with her Sir Gerald. The divorce would cause a scandal, but in the fickle minds of society, such things were quickly forgotten. He should have chosen someone like Lady Loretta Macdonald to be his bride, someone mature and poised.

He became aware that all eyes had turned to the doorway and that people were chattering and whispering with excitement. "What's the commotion about?" drawled Lady Macdonald. "Has Prinny arrived?"

The duke, with his commanding height, looked over the intervening heads. Standing in the doorway, being welcomed by the Sandwells, was his wife. She looked radiant and happy. She looked young and fresh and very beautiful. Beside her, like some sort of squat guardian watchdog, stood Mrs. Duggan, her small periwinkle eyes roaming this way and that as she appreciated the sensation her beautiful companion was causing in the room.

The waltz was announced. "Our dance, I think," said Lady Macdonald at his elbow.

He murmured something but kept looking at Alice. Someone asked her to dance, a tall guardsman, splendid in his scarlet regimentals. Alice smiled up at him and floated off in his arms. The duke could not believe that the sight of his wife performing the waltz with anyone else should cause him such pain.

"I did not think you an admirer of Prinny," mocked Lady Macdonald. "Or rather, I assume that is the reason all are gossiping and staring."

"My wife has arrived," said the duke, and, putting his arm around Lady Macdonald's waist, he led her off in the steps of the dance.

Lady Macdonald was merely amused. Scandal was what was causing the buzz of excitement in the room. She had seen Alice once at a distance and had damned her as a provincial miss.

But as the duke swung her round, she had a perfect view of the Duchess of Ferrant and bit back an exclamation of dismay. The duchess was beautiful, with a rare, fresh beauty not often seen in the overheated ballrooms and saloons of fashionable London. The duke, normally an expert dancer, stepped on her toes and muttered an apology. She looked up at him and saw his eyes were fixed on his wife. Lady Macdonald felt a stab of fear. Up until that little duchess had arrived, the road had lain clear before her. He would get a divorce and she would become the duchess. She had heard the gossip about Sir Gerald Warby and had enjoyed it immensely but never for one moment considered this wife to be a rival in any way. Lady Macdonald was thirty, but she enjoyed all the license and freedom of a widow and the admiration of many courtiers—and so she was able to forget her age and feel that in beauty, she reigned supreme. Under the mask of her makeup, her face hardened. Something would have to be done.

The duke felt he simply had to speak to his wife to find out why she had defied his instructions, forgetting that these instructions, conveyed to Alice by his secretary, had merely been put as a suggestion that they did not attend the same events. But her hand was eagerly sought for each dance. He was furious that she appeared to be enjoying herself immensely. He was obliged to take Lady Macdonald into supper, but that lady had little pleasure in his company, for he answered all her flirtatious remarks automatically, his eyes always sliding in the direction of Alice, who was sitting with that wretched guardsman and laughing at something he was saying.

Alice met Mrs. Duggan as she was leaving the supper room. "Time to go," whispered Mrs. Duggan.

"But why?"

"He's been trying to secure a dance with you, talk to you. Now let him look for you."

"But he does not even appear to have noticed me!"

"He noticed you. Now we beat a tactical retreat."

As Alice climbed down from her carriage outside the duke's town house, Mrs. Duggan leaned forward. "He will no doubt call on you this night to berate you about something or other. Be cool and dignified. *He* is now the one that is in the wrong. Don't forget that. Oh, and I am getting up a little party of friends to go to Vauxhall tomorrow night. Come with us. Don't let him see you sitting about the place, pining."

"Very well," said Alice, "but he has never called on me before."

However, mindful of the Irishwoman's remarks, Alice put on her prettiest nightgown and a lacy confection of a nightcap and lay in bed reading, waiting all the while for the sound of her husband's footsteps on the stairs. At last, she heard him coming home. She felt a stab of fear and wondered whether to feign sleep, but then she decided to face him. But although she heard him slowly mount the stairs and hesitate at the top, he turned off to his own quarters. Feeling sad and relieved at the same time, Alice blew out the candle beside the bed, drew the curtains, and fell asleep.

She awoke late in the morning and stretched and yawned and drew back the bed curtains. And then she fell back against the pillows with a little gasp, drawing the blankets protectively up to her chin, for her husband was sitting on a chair beside the bed.

"What do you want?" asked Alice, fighting down her nervousness and remembering Mrs. Duggan's words that the duke was now the guilty one. "Have you been waiting there long?" she added in a milder voice. "You should have told Betty to wake me."

"I came in only a few moments ago," he said. He was in his undress, a long banyan of cloth of gold wrapped about him over a nightgown trimmed with more lace than Alice's own. "I wish to speak to you."

Alice settled herself more comfortably against the pillows and regarded him steadily. "What about?"

"I thought we had more or less agreed to attend separate functions."

"I will do so in future. Had I known the reason was because you wished to attend certain events with your mistress, Lady Macdonald, then I would not have changed my plans."

"How dare you! Lady Macdonald is a friend."

Alice blinked at him and said, with pretty surprise, "La, sir. When a gentleman squires a lady of overblown looks, immodest dress, and doubtful morals about London, the gossips will chatter so.

But I see now you have only been kind to an aging lady long past the first blush of youth."

"You little hellcat. Have you no shame for your own behavior?"

"That was in the past," said Alice calmly, although her heart was hammering. "Lady Macdonald is in the present. I am to attend Vauxhall this evening with Mrs. Duggan. I tell you that in case you fear we might meet."

"I have no fear of our meeting socially."

"Then what is this conversation about? Ferrant, if you are trying to tell me that you wish to divorce me and marry Lady Macdonald, please say so and stop this tiresome sparring."

Amazement flickered in his eyes. Where was the crushed Alice, the guilty Alice now?

"I do not wish to discuss such weighty matters before breakfast," he said, his voice sounding unbearably pompous to his own ears.

"As you wish," said Alice politely.

He gave her a baffled look and rose and stalked from the room.

Alice lay still after he had gone, fear warring with a certain triumph in her bosom. They had crossed swords, but, oh, how much better *that* was than to creep about this great mansion, frightened of meeting him.

The duke went to his club that afternoon. He had promised to take Lady Macdonald to the opera that evening. For the first time he began to worry about Lady Macdonald's thoughts. She could surely not expect to marry him. And yet, that was an idea he had been toying with since he first met her.

Edward Vere was lounging in a chair in front of

the fire in the coffee room. "Delighted to see you," he cried when he saw the duke. "My poor Lucy is not very well and I have been sent out."

"What is the matter?" asked the duke sharply. "Have you called for the physician?"

"Lucy is being sick in the mornings, due to her condition, or so I'm told, but it worries me greatly."

"Congratulations. So you are to be a father."

"Do you think it will be a boy?" asked Edward anxiously. "Should I put his name down for a good regiment?"

"Too premature," said the duke, with a laugh. "It might be a girl."

"A girl! Well, that would be splendid, too. I shall be quite the doting father whatever comes along. Did you ever think to see me married?"

"No, in truth, I thought you would remain a bachelor."

"That was until I saw my Lucy. How goes Alice?"

"Well, I thank you."

"Heard she was belle of the ball last night. Fellows are writing poems about her." Edward shifted uncomfortably in his chair. "In fact, lots of gossip about that ball."

"Ah ... and are the gossips saying that I was there with Lady Macdonald?"

"Well, yes."

"*Tcha!* I do not care what the gossips say."

"You don't? Demme, the way you've been going on since your wedding one would think you cared for little else," exclaimed Edward.

"Explain yourself."

"No, I won't. Work it out for yourself. I ain't telling you, for you'd only call me out—and I have a mind to live long enough to see my child! Your affairs are your business."

"Exactly."

"So let's have a bottle of port and talk about something else."

Chapter Four

It was not Alice's first visit to Vauxhall, but it was turning out to be the most enjoyable one she had experienced. In Mrs. Duggan's party were two young Irishmen, Lord Dunfear and Mr. Donnelly, both easygoing rattles who paid her such extravagant compliments, they made her laugh. Lord Dunfear was tall and gangling and Mr. Donnelly was small and black-haired, with those intense blue Irish eyes fringed with heavy black lashes.

They listened to the music, promenaded in the walks under the lanterns, and then returned to their box for supper, where Mr. Donnelly tried to demonstrate his expertise in juggling with two wineglasses and a fork and dropped all of them—and looked so outraged that Alice giggled.

And that was how Sir Gerald Warby saw her. She was simply dressed in a white muslin gown with a blue silk pelisse and was wearing a frivolous confection of ribbons and flowers in her hair.

He had been strolling along with a noisy party of bloods, but with a hurried excuse, he detached himself from his party and approached the box.

Before Alice had even introduced him, Mrs. Duggan could tell by her blush and sparkling eyes that this was Sir Gerald Warby. Mrs. Duggan looked at him in surprise, for how could such a man even begin to compete with Alice's husband? He had a handsome face, but it was marred by a rather weak and sensual mouth. His clothes were of the best, but the diamond in his cravat was made of paste.

Alice, after the introductions had been made, asked him to join them. He entertained the company with some of his adventures abroad and then, when Mrs. Duggan turned to talk to the two Irishmen, he said in a low voice to Alice, "How can you ever forgive me? Walk with me for a little and I will explain."

"There is no need for explanations," said Alice, with a lightness she did not feel. "You forget I am a married lady."

"An unhappily married lady, if the gossips have it aright."

"I never listen to gossip," said Alice coldly. "My marriage is no concern of yours, sir."

He put his hand on his heart. "Would that it were," he breathed.

Alice felt uncomfortable. There was something very stagy about that gesture. Her initial rapture at seeing him was fading fast. She was now more experienced in the ways of the world than when she had first met him. And he had changed in a subtle way. There was a glittering, hectic look in his black eyes and he smelled strongly of the Gardens' rack punch and tobacco smoke.

"I am feeling faint," said Mrs. Duggan, looking remarkably hale and healthy. "Forgive me, but I must go home."

Alice immediately rose to her feet. "We will all go," she said, picking up her fan and reticule. "My apologies, Sir Gerald."

He bowed over her hand and said huskily, "I shall call on you tomorrow."

Alice withdrew her hand and said gently, "No, that would not be wise. Good night, sir."

Gerald sat on in the box and finished the rack punch. He was joined by his friends.

"So that's the Duchess of Ferrant," said one. "Had I such a charmer as a bride, I would not waste my time on Lady Macdonald."

Sir Gerald sobered on the spot. "Who?" he demanded, and then listened eagerly. When they had finished, he lay back in his chair, his eyes half-closed, and thought hard. He had led a rackety life abroad and had become greedy for money to satisfy his desires of high living and gambling. He had almost run through the generous amount of money paid to him by Alice's parents to stay away. Alice must have changed. She was no longer a virgin . . . and it was well known that unhappy wives in London society took lovers. If he could enjoy her favors and then somehow let Mr. and Mrs. Lacey know about it, perhaps they might pay him again.

The following day, Sir Gerald waited across the road from the duke's town house until he saw him driving out. Then straightening his beaver hat, he strode across the road.

A haughty butler opened the door. Sir Gerald confidently presented his card and asked for an audience with the duchess. The butler put the card on a silver salver and mounted the stairs. Gerald waited eagerly. After what seemed too long a time, the butler came back. "Her Grace is not at home," he said.

Gerald could not believe she would not see him. "When will she return?" he asked.

"I do not know," said the butler stonily.

There was nothing else for Gerald to do but take his leave.

He went to a coffeehouse in Pall Mall, wondering what to do next. Then he thought of this Lady Macdonald. Would it be possible to get her to help him? By asking about among his friends, he secured her address and went there.

He was told that Lady Macdonald did not rise until four in the afternoon. Gerald looked at his pocket watch. It was quarter past three.

"I will wait," he said grimly.

He was shown into a saloon on the ground floor, a little-used saloon from the look of it, the sort of room where doubtful callers were placed instead of being taken upstairs to one of the less public rooms.

There was a French clock on the mantelpiece. He watched impatiently as the minutes ticked by. Finally at four o'clock exactly the door opened and the butler said, "If you would be so good as to follow me, sir."

For one short moment before he mounted the stairs, Gerald remembered a younger, cleaner, more hopeful Gerald who, for a brief, heady time, had been deeply and sweetly in love with Alice Lacey. But debts and social snubs had crept in between, souring his disposition, making him feel like a spoiled child whose glittering toys had been snatched away from him by a cruel fate.

His eyes gleamed when he saw Lady Loretta Macdonald. She was in her undress, a lacy wrapper over a lacy nightdress. Her flaming hair, thick and shining with oil, cascaded down on her white shoulders.

"Such beauty," murmured Gerald, kissing her hand.

"Charmed," she said in her throaty voice. "I do not think we are acquainted. State the reason for your call."

"I will be brutally frank," said Sir Gerald, flipping up the long tails of his coat and sinking down into an armchair opposite her. "I am in love with Alice, Duchess of Ferrant."

"So!" Her eyes widened slightly. "I have heard gossip about you, that the little duchess's pet bird cried out your name on the day of her wedding. But what is that to me?"

"I have heard that the Duke of Ferrant is courting you."

"Indeed. Many men court me, Sir Gerald."

"Of course, of course. But do you hope to marry Ferrant?"

"That is my business, not yours."

"I think you could do with my help."

"Sir Gerald, I find you impertinent."

"Alas, it is my love for Alice . . . I mean the duchess, that has made me so bold."

She studied him in silence for a moment. Then she said slowly, "And how could you help?"

"I am sure I could reanimate the duchess's affections toward me. I met the lady at Vauxhall last night." He kissed his fingertips. "What a welcome! Ferrant is a proud man. It is all right for him to be unfaithful, but what duke would tolerate similar behavior in his own wife?"

"And yet such things go on," murmured Lady Macdonald.

"In a couple so newly wed and without the heir to the dukedom being secured?"

"And all you want in return is the love of the duchess?"

"As to that," he said awkwardly, "I find myself sadly short of the readies . . . and that is a certain barrier to courting the duchess."

She threw back her head and laughed. Then she looked at him, her eyes glittering with amusement. "A man after my own heart. So we are talking business, hey?"

Gerald spread his hands in a deprecatory gesture.

"Well, I shall look on it as an investment," said Lady Macdonald. "But see you do your work well. I make a bad enemy." She rose and crossed to a desk, then sat down and began to write busily.

Then she rose and handed him a slip of paper. "That is a draft on my bank." Gerald blinked at the large sum. "Now, shall we discuss strategy? It is time your little duchess saw me with Ferrant again. Miss Taylor is to have her come-out ball tomorrow night. Although the family is not *bon* ton, Ferrant has agreed to go because the father is an old army friend. He is taking me. It is up to us to see the duchess goes. I myself will engineer an invitation for you, and I will tell Mr. Taylor that it is Ferrant's wish that his wife should accept an invitation. I believe Taylor discreetly did not send her one. You play your part and I will play mine."

Alice duly received a pressing invitation from Mr. Taylor to attend his daughter's ball. In his letter he said he was an old friend of her husband's. Alice showed the letter to Mrs. Duggan, along with the accompanying invitation card. "Very strange," said Mrs. Duggan. "I myself have an invitation, but then, I have known the Taylors this age. Had you anything else planned for this evening?"

Alice shook her head. "I planned to go to bed early. Madame Duval is going to spend most of this afternoon fitting me for all sorts of ensembles."

"But nothing ready yet? No? Then she had better refurbish something for this evening, for it is my belief you should go."

"What if Ferrant is there with Lady Macdonald?"

"All to the better. To arrive escorting one's mistress when one's wife is present is just not done."

"What if Sir Gerald Warby is there?"

Mrs. Duggan looked at her thoughtfully. She wanted to say that such as Sir Gerald was not a patch on Ferrant, but she said instead, "He is not invited anywhere much." Mrs. Duggan had been making inquiries. "But Lord Dunfear and young Donnelly are to attend. I suggest they escort us. You will therefore have two safe partners, and one of them will escort you to supper."

The butler entered. "Lord Werford and his son, the Honorable Percy Burke," he announced.

"I do not think I know them," said Alice.

"If it pleases Your Grace, Lord Werford is His Grace's second cousin."

"In that case, I had better see them. Is His Grace not at home?"

"No, Your Grace."

"Then you may show them in."

The duke's relative was older than the duke by at least twenty years. He was a small, swarthy man with a yellowish complexion, which could mean either that he had spent some time in India, or, what was more likely, there was something up with his liver. He had heavy eyebrows, bulging eyes, and a yapping voice. His son was also small but very neat—neat little features, neat little figure, finicky, precise movements.

"You must excuse my bad memory," said Alice. "I do not remember you at the wedding."

"Traveling abroad," barked Lord Werford. "Both of us. Grand Tour. Boy's education. Important."

"Quite. May I present Mrs. Duggan. Mrs. Duggan, Lord Werford and the Honorable Percy Burke."

Lord Werford bowed jerkily, but the Honorable Percy swept out a huge silk handkerchief and waved it in the air in a series of descending swoops, bowing as he did so, until his nose almost reached the floor. And then he stayed motionless, doubled up.

"Do rise, sir," said Alice, stifling a giggle. "I am not the queen."

"But you are the queen of beauty," said Percy, straightening up. "One glance from your eyes has pierced my heart."

"I don't like you," said Oracle suddenly, from his cage in the corner of the drawing room. "I don't like you *at all*."

Alice blushed guiltily. She had been talking to the bird recently about Lady Macdonald, ending up by crying, "I don't like you at all, my lady." Oracle had omitted the "my lady," and so it sounded uncannily as if the bird had taken a dislike to the guests.

"Do excuse my pet," she said. "He parrots odd phrases that mean nothing."

"If that were my bird," said Lord Werford, puffing out his cheeks in anger, "I would have him shot. Shot on the spot, ma'am."

The mynah began to laugh, swinging backward and forward on its perch, a devilish laugh, a laugh from hell. Oh, dear, thought Alice, who now knew all the members of her husband's large staff. That must be Evans. Evans was one of the housemaids, quick and efficient at her work but possessed of a really evil laugh. Alice had heard that laugh once— sounding up from the servants' quarters—and had asked the butler, Hoskins, who on earth was possessed of a laugh like that.

Lord Werford strutted up to the cage. "Be quiet," he roared.

"Shan't, shan't, shan't," shouted the mynah. Lord Werford backed away and crossed himself.

Mrs. Tembil's spoiled brat of a child, thought Alice, remembering a painful visit by a society matron. "The bird is not speaking to you, Lord Werford. It is merely stringing together odd phrases. Now may I offer you some refreshment?"

Oracle fell mercifully silent while Alice entertained Lord Werford and his son with cakes and wine. Mrs. Duggan chattered on about this and that and Alice was glad of it, as father and son studied her the whole time in an unnerving way; she was glad when the couple at last rose to leave.

Percy asked her to go driving with him and, when Alice explained that the afternoon was going to be taken up with fittings, he made a very long and embarrassing speech about the folly of gilding the lily, until his father edged him toward the door.

"Goodness!" said Alice when they had left. "The next time they call, I hope Ferrant is at home."

* * *

The duke paused on his way out that evening. "Hoskins," he said, "have there been any callers on the duchess today?"

"Yes, Your Grace. Lord Werford and the Honorable Percy."

"The deuce! What did that old fool want?"

"His Lordship wished to present his compliments to the duchess."

"Indeed! Anyone else?"

"Mrs. Duggan and then the dressmaker, Madame Duval."

"And that is all?"

"All that Her Grace would receive."

"You interest me. Whom would she not receive?"

"Sir Gerald Warby, Your Grace."

"Thank you, Hoskins. That will be all."

So, thought the duke as he walked out to his carriage, his little bride was behaving just as she ought. He thought of the evening ahead and felt uncomfortable. He had enjoyed his light flirtation with Lady Macdonald, had even, just recently, toyed with the idea of divorcing Alice and marrying her instead. But at the opera, Lady Macdonald had begun to assume a proprietorial air that he did not like.

He had to admit that the wantonness of her dress, which had so charmed him, had begun to appear vulgar. And yet when he called at her home to escort her to the ball, the very respectability of her gown on this occasion alarmed him. Lady Macdonald was already beginning to behave as if she were the duchess, rather than Alice. Instead of feeling in control of things, instead of feeling he was punishing Alice, he felt very much in the wrong, very much like just another London roué hell-bent on shaming his wife. But none of these disturbing thoughts showed through the polite mask of his face.

He reflected bitterly that since he had become a duke, he had become used to thinking that everything that he did was above censure, and he had been helped in that, he thought, by London society, who toadied to him quite dreadfully. And so he was taking his mistress to an old friend's daughter's ball, and, up until that moment, had not thought much about the enormity of his behavior. He had been so hurt by Alice, so humiliated. He had treated her like glass during their engagement, never pressing kisses or embraces on her. Edward and Lucy were to be at the Taylors this evening—Edward, who had asked him not to do anything so tactless as to introduce Lady Macdonald to Lucy, "for she's in a delicate condition," he had said awkwardly, "and I do not want to do anything to upset her."

The fact that the duke was in a very bad mood, indeed, did not communicate itself to Lady Macdonald, who was so narcissistic that her pleasure in her own beauty had armored her effectively from the feelings of others. To spend an evening in her company, she judged, was an event of such high order than no man could fail to be delighted.

It was perhaps unfortunate that the Taylors had decided to enlarge the appearance of their saloon, where the ball was being held, by having long sheets of looking glass along the walls.

Alice was performing the quadrille with Mr. Donnelly. She was facing one of these sheets of mirror when Lady Macdonald entered, and so the duke had a perfect reflection of himself and Lady Macdonald—and also of Alice and Mr. Donnelly. Lady Macdonald's reflected face wore an uncharacteristic look of sour uneasiness. Alice was smiling at Mr. Donnelly, the thin folds of yet another gauze overdress, this one spangled with gold, floating out from her body. Her hair was soft and gleaming and held in place with two delicate stems of gold corn. She looked very fresh and lovely. Mr. Donnelly, with his black curls and merry blue eyes, was, the duke judged, as young as Alice. He felt old and dirty.

His eyes turned back to where Mr. Taylor was standing at the door with his wife, and Mr. Taylor mouthed ruefully, "Not my fault."

And then to add to the duke's sourness, Sir Gerald Warby was announced.

The gossips were having a field day. Fans were raised over painted faces and voices hissed and whispered while Alice and the reflected Alice danced on, apparently without a care in the world.

Alice saw the duke, but her steps did not falter. She had also seen Sir Gerald Warby. "Sure, we'll not be letting the fellow near you," murmured Mr. Donnelly.

Left to her own devices, Alice would have found it hard to avoid Sir Gerald. He was persistent in trying to secure a dance with her. But anytime he tried to approach her, she always managed to elude him by accepting the hand of the nearest gentleman who asked her to dance. Across the room, he saw Lady Macdonald sending him a gimlet look.

The duke heartily wished the evening over. He could not help noticing the deft way Alice avoided Sir Gerald, or the way Mrs. Duggan directed those two Irishmen, Donnelly and Dunfear, to Alice's side when it looked as if Sir Gerald were about to come too close to her. *He* should have been the one to protect his own wife.

While Lady Macdonald was dancing with a dazed-looking youth, he took the opportunity to ask Mr. Taylor, "Why did you ask my wife?"

"Demme, that was Lady Macdonald's idea. Loretta said you wanted your wife to have an invitation. I thought that Loretta did not mean to attend. I did not know she was mischief-making."

"Nor I."

He waited until Lady Macdonald had finished dancing and then approached her. "We are leaving," he said abruptly.

"So soon?" The eyes that looked into his were searching and wary.

He forced himself to smile. He did not want to have a scene with her in the ballroom. "I would be private with you," he murmured.

She gave a slow smile of triumph. Her moment had arrived. She would have him in her bed . . . and then at the altar.

But no sooner were they seated in the privacy of his carriage than the duke said, "What prompted you to tell Taylor to insist on my wife's attendance?"

"As to that, Sir Gerald Warby is back in Town, and it is known your little wife is enamored of him. Do not look so!" Lady Macdonald studied his grim face anxiously in the bobbing light of the carriage lamp. "Surely what is sauce for the goose is sauce for the gander. Everyone in society accepts us as a couple."

"I have behaved very badly," he said. "To you, and to my wife. It must stop." His lips curved in a bitter smile. "If I have led you to believe that my intentions were other than dishonorable, then I beg you to forgive me for that, too."

"What is this?" she demanded, fanning herself vigorously. "The great Duke of Ferrant is content to be cuckolded by his own wife?"

"You go too far. My wife was indeed at one time in love with Sir Gerald. I would not have married her at all had her parents not misled me as to the nature of her affections. Loretta, all this is very painful. You should never have interfered. To have managed to get both my wife and Warby—yes, I am sure you were behind his invitation as well—to this ball was a cruel trick on all concerned, and the person who is perhaps going to be most hurt by the outcome is you yourself."

"Ferrant, forgive me. What was I to do? You showed all you preferred me to your milksop of a wife. What else could I think? I thought if you saw her together with Sir Gerald, it might prompt you to action, to divorce."

"It did not work," he said heavily. "I behaved disgracefully . . . and my wife behaved just as she ought."

"Damn her." Lady Macdonald clutched the fan in her hand so hard that the ivory sticks snapped.

"We have not been lovers," he said in a conciliatory tone. "We can still be friends despite the trick you have played on me."

She forced herself to smile. The game was not over so long as she still had access to him.

"I thank you," she said. "Your friendship is of great value to me."

Alice had noticed him leave with Lady Macdonald, had noticed the triumphant smile on that lady's face, and had found herself hard put to remain apparently cheerful. She was half tempted to escape from her guard and talk to Sir Gerald. Sir Gerald had loved her. But somehow she could not recapture the soft memories of that first love. Sir Gerald had spent some time in the card room, gambling and drinking, once he had seen there was no hope of getting near her. He had just come back to the ballroom. He looked much older and harder, and, with a little feeling of emotional treachery, she could not help noticing that he was a trifle short in the leg.

The headache she had thought of pleading to as an excuse to go home became a reality. Mrs. Duggan, noticing her white face and glittering eyes, readily agreed to go as well, and Mr. Donnelly and Lord Dunfear escorted them.

Outside the duke's house, she politely invited them in for refreshment, but Mrs. Duggan said soothingly that she had done very well and should go straight to bed.

A footman who had been on the backstrap of the carriage had already hammered on the great door for admittance, and another footman was letting down the carriage steps. Betty, Alice's maid, silently walked behind her mistress, carrying her fan and reticule.

Alice had been brought up surrounded by servants and so was used to them, but in that moment, she wished she could be somewhere entirely alone. Watching servants meant one could not betray any emotion—a lady never did so in any case—and for the first time Alice felt this lack of privacy acutely.

When she reached her quarters, she dismissed Betty, saying she had a mind to put herself to bed.

Betty studied her mistress's face and then curtsied obediently and withdrew.

Wearily Alice sat down at the toilet table, took the gold ornaments from her hair, and began to brush it with long strokes.

The door behind her opened and her husband stood on the threshold. She stared at his reflection in the round mirror in front of her, the brush poised.

"It is late," he said, coming into the room and closing the door behind him. "But I would like to talk to you."

Alice swung round on the stool. "Yes, Ferrant," she said wearily.

He was formidable and remote in impeccable evening dress, dark blue coat, white waistcoat, white cravat, dark blue silk knee breeches, and clocked stockings. A dark red ruby blazed from among the snowy folds of his cravat and a larger ruby burned with somber red fire from an antique ring he wore on his middle finger.

Those odd, slightly slanting eyes of his studied her for a moment. His hair gleamed guinea gold in the wavering candlelight.

He pulled forward a chair and sat down, stretching out his legs, which were long enough to please even Alice's mother.

"That was an unfortunate evening," he said.

Alice sat, very still, waiting for him to go on.

"I shall explain matters like this. You were, I believe, in love with Sir Gerald Warby."

Alice winced.

"I am not going to berate you. Do you love him still?"

"No. No, I don't," said Alice, the naive note of

surprise in her voice betraying the truth of her statement.

"But I assume he was your first love. I want you to remember the sweetness of that for this reason. You, Alice, were *my* first love, and I loved you deeply and tenderly . . . and I never thought that you did not love me. I thought that only poets believed that love was blind. But think on that and then realize what my feelings were when I found you, on our wedding day, with Sir Gerald in the rose garden."

"I am bitterly ashamed of myself," said Alice in a low voice.

"But indulging in recriminations will not help us," he went on. "I have not made Lady Macdonald my mistress. I flirted with her, yes, and I admit I was fascinated with her, but underneath it all I hoped to cause you as much pain as you had caused me. Tonight, I saw how ridiculous all these games were. I told Lady Macdonald that any feelings on my part toward her would, in future, be nothing other than friendship. This is a marriage in name only, Alice, but at least we can preserve our dignity. Do you agree?"

"Yes, oh, yes," said Alice shyly.

"Then I will trouble you no more on the subject."

"Society is malicious, Ferrant. Should you hear any rumors against me, please come to me with them rather than believe them, I beg of you."

"That is a promise."

Alice hesitated, and then said in a rush, "I, too, have been behaving badly. I have been ordering a great deal of expensive gowns and trinkets."

He smiled. "I should hope you would. You are allowed to enjoy yourself."

Emboldened, Alice said, "The drawing room is very depressing. Would it be possible . . . could I . . . refurnish it?"

"Of course. Ask my secretary. He will cope with the bills and tell you the best places to order what you want. Now, good night. Tomorrow is a new beginning."

He raised her hand and kissed it and left the room.

Alice mechanically prepared for bed. She could not help turning what he had said over and over in her head—of how he had loved her, of how he *had* loved her—and she sadly felt that she had once owned something very valuable without ever guessing its true worth.

Chapter Five

WHEN SHE CALLED the following afternoon, Mrs. Duggan was pleased to see that her pretty friend, instead of being cast down, was busy studying books of paint colors with the duke's young secretary, Mr. Shadwell.

"As you see," said Alice gaily, "I have set about refurbishing the drawing room. If you could order the paint we have chosen, Mr. Shadwell, and engage the decorators, we can decide on the new furniture later."

The young man bowed and withdrew. "Well?" demanded the Irishwoman eagerly. "You are in fine spirits."

"All is resolved," said Alice. "Ferrant has apologized for Lady Macdonald and we are to make the best of things. I feel as if an enormous weight of guilt has been lifted from my shoulders. And yet I am not going to the opera tonight, for I feel sure Lady Macdonald will be there and I do not want to see her."

"Does Ferrant go?"

A shadow crossed Alice's face. "I do not know." She had hoped that her husband might begin their fresh life together by discussing his plans for the day, but her maid had told her that he had left early to ride in the Row and had not returned.

"So what can we do to amuse you?" asked Mrs. Duggan. "Donnelly and Dunfear are at our service."

Alice glanced out of the long windows, where the sun was blazing down on the sooty London streets. "Such a fine day. Do you know, I would like to go on the river. Does it cost very much?" she added, not wishing to put their escorts to any great expense.

"Not a bit of it, unless the rogues try to cheat us. Crossing above London Bridge is twopence per person, and below the bridge is a penny each. A whole boat to Windsor is two shillings per person. We have not time to sail that far, but we could take a boat a little way upstream. I shall scribble a note and one of your footmen can run to Dunfear's lodgings with it. Donnelly is residing with him. Wear a warm cloak, for it can become chilly on the water."

In an hour's time, they were standing at London Bridge Stair, at the end of a line of people waiting for boats. The watermen each wore their Doggett's coat and badge as a sign that they were legally authorized to ply their trade and that they were expected to act on a "first come, first served" basis. But the greedy watermen scanned the line, looking for the most prosperous. To Alice's dismay, they were claimed by a rough fellow ahead of shabbier-looking passengers who were waiting patiently in line, but Lord Dunfear said cheerfully it was the way of the world and ushered the party on board a rowing boat without a qualm of conscience.

Alice was enchanted to be out on the water

among the scudding sculls and the brown sails of the hoys. Stately black and gold aldermen's barges ploughed past. The river was crowded. Ships lay at anchor in midstream, discharging cargo and passengers, which necessitated a busy fleet of lighters and barges. The Pool of London was a forest of bobbing masts. Above the busy scene, the dome of St. Paul's seemed to swim in the golden light. Government barges belonging to the customs and admiralty were as brave as gold and color could make them, the customs boats making their annual pilgrimage to the Trinity almshouses at Deptford Strand, all the people on board being armed with huge bouquets and bags of fancy cakes and biscuits. The river had an air of holiday. The banks of the river were lined with manufactories and warehouses: iron founders, dyers, soap and oil makers, glass makers, shot makers, and boat builders. In between the factories, crazy wooden tenements, teeming with life, hung over the river, the rickety edifices looking on the point of collapse.

The waterman rowed them up and down while they chatted and watched the busy scene—until a cool little breeze blew up and Mrs. Duggan pulled her shawl more tightly about her shoulders and suggested they should return.

But as they disembarked at London Bridge Stairs, the waterman demanded five shillings. "What!" exclaimed Lord Dunfear, turning red with embarrassment because he only had three shillings in his pockets and doubted whether his friend, Mr. Donnelly, had any money at all. "I shall give you two shillings, fellow," he said loftily, "and count yourself lucky."

" 'Ere!" shouted the waterman to his fellows. "This 'ere buck is a-cheating of me."

A nasty-looking crowd of watermen began to crowd round.

"Oh, let me pay the man," said Mrs. Duggan.

"No," said Lord Dunfear, looking scared but determined. "Nobody's going to take me for a flat."

The waterman, a burly fellow built like an ape, spat on his hands and approached the cringing lord. "You'll pay me and be glad of it," he snarled.

Young Mr. Donnelly sprang in front of his friend and put his fists up. "You'll fight me first," he said.

"What is this?" demanded an acid voice.

The crowd of watermen and spectators parted and the Duke of Ferrant strode to the front of the crowd. He was in his riding dress and top boots. His hair under his curly-brimmed beaver shone in the sunlight and he carried a gold-topped cane under one arm.

Alice breathlessly explained that the waterman was asking for too much money and had been offered two shillings, which he had refused to accept. The duke asked how long they had been on the water and then looked down from his great height at the squat and burly waterman. "Two shillings is a generous sum," he said.

The waterman's eyes gleamed as he took in the duke's magnificence. "So *you* fight me," he said, with a grin.

To Alice's horror, the duke gave a curt nod and began to remove his coat. She had led a very protected life and did not know that in London, rank did not protect the aristocrat, who could be called on to fight by anyone who felt like it, something that appalled the emigrant French aristocrats.

"Ferrant, please don't," she whispered. "He will kill you."

"I doubt it," he said, with a smile. "He wants a fight, not a murder."

Mrs. Duggan drew Alice back. The crowd was thickening. Lord Dunfear made a token protest, as did Mr. Donnelly, but both could not hide their immense relief that it was the duke who was going to take the punishment for them. The duke, in shirtsleeves and hatless, faced up to his adversary.

The waterman smashed a fist into the duke's ribs, and the duke danced back and then began to hit out. Alice turned and buried her face in Mrs. Duggan's ample bosom. Then she heard the sound of a terrific blow, followed by a sickening thud, and then a long silence. Then a great cheer went up. She opened her eyes. The watermen were throwing their caps in the air and cheering. Shuddering she looked down, expecting to see the duke stretched on the ground. But it was the waterman who lay there and, miraculously, his fellows were cheering the winning duke.

The duke put on his coat and hat as his adversary groggily sat up rubbing his chin. The duke tossed him a sovereign. "More than you deserve," he said, "but you are a good fighter."

And to more cheers from the watermen and the crowd, the duke took Alice's arm and shepherded her to his carriage. "Hoskins told me you had gone to the river," he said, "so I came in pursuit of you."

"I don't understand," said Alice, bewildered. "I thought he would kill you! And why were his friends cheering *you*?"

"Because they like a fight and always cheer the winner. They are not bad fellows. If you want to go on the river in future, you had better let me arrange it."

"I closed my eyes after he hit you," said Alice. "Are you hurt?"

"I shall be a bit stiff and sore for the next few days, but I shall come about. What are your plans for the evening? The opera?"

He noticed a shadow cross Alice's face. "No," she said awkwardly. "I planned to spend a quiet evening at home."

He wondered whether it would be a good idea to stay at home himself, to get to know his wife better. But she was very shy of him. An evening of stilted conversation would not help matters.

"How dull," he said lightly. "We could go to Richmond for supper by the river and take your Irish friends with us," and without waiting for her reply, he turned and issued the invitation, which was received with enthusiasm. The duke was glad to see that both the Irishmen regarded Alice as a friend. There was no sign of anything warmer.

The expedition was agreed on and all parties, for different reasons well satisfied, went home to change.

Lord Werford and the Honorable Percy Burke were waiting for a visit from Sir Gerald Warby while the duke and his party set out for Richmond. "Do you think he will come?" asked Percy fretfully.

"Bound to," said Lord Werford. "Told him there was money in it for him."

"Are you sure the stories about him and the duchess are true?"

"Had it from a most respectable source."

"There he is," said Percy, hearing a murmur of voices from belowstairs.

"Now, leave the talking to me," said Lord Werford.

Sir Gerald was announced. The elaborate ritual of bows, handkerchief flourishing, snuffbox snapping had to be gone through before Sir Gerald sat down and looked at the pair curiously. "What is your pleasure gentlemen?" he asked.

"Hear you're in love with the Duchess of Ferrant," said Lord Werford.

"Alas, she is wed to another," sighed Gerald.

Percy went to the window and stood looking down into the street as if disengaging himself from the proceedings.

"Not necessarily," barked Lord Werford.

Gerald, unused to his lordship's elliptical method of talking, said, "I beg your pardon?"

"Ferrant dies. Get the widow."

"Lord Werford, much as it distresses me to point out such an obvious fact, Ferrant is in the prime of life and as fit as a flea."

Lord Werford laid a finger alongside his nose. "Accidents do happen."

Gerald looked at him, his black eyes narrowed to calculating slits. "Let me see," he said, "if Ferrant dies, who inherits?"

"Him," said Lord Werford, ungrammatically but succinctly, jerking a thumb at Percy, whose neat little shoulders gave an infinitesimal shrug.

"Ah. What sort of accident?"

"Accidents will happen," said Lord Werford. "Oh, riding accidents, bits of masonry falling, guns popping off all over the place these days—antiwar riots, bread riots, Irish thugs wanting their country . . . lots of things."

"And you are prepared to wait and see if one of these . . . er . . . accidents happens?" asked Gerald.

"We thought you might be interested in helping fate."

"And how much is my interest worth?"

"A king's ransom. A tenth of the dukedom."

"Let us not beat about the bush." Gerald leaned forward. "You are prepared to pay me a vast sum for murdering Ferrant?"

"Trifle blunt put like that. But, yes."

"And if I refuse?"

"That's that, I suppose." Lord Werford leaned back in his chair, but Gerald was aware of Percy turning round from the window. There was a heavy air of menace in the room.

So, the hard fact is, I take the offer or they murder me, thought Gerald.

"Let me think," he said aloud. He calculated, as they sat there and watched him, that he could at least try. If he failed, however . . .

"To show goodwill," he said cautiously, "you would need to pay money in advance."

"We have already thought of that. Ten thousand pounds."

All scruples fled from Gerald's brain. With ten thousand pounds, he could flee the country if the undertaking appeared to be too difficult. And he wanted Alice. With a tenth of the value of the dukedom, he could have Alice and all his pleasures as well.

"Agreed," he said.

"There is one other thing to consider, however," said Percy suddenly. "Gossip has it that the couple live separate lives. My man is walking out with one of the maids from Ferrant's town house and says this is the case. It is well known that Ferrant is having an intrigue with Lady Macdonald. And yet a rumor has just reached us that perhaps Ferrant has ended his relationship with Lady Macdonald. At the Taylors' ball, it was noted that he kept watching his wife. You will need to move quickly. If the couple become reconciled to each other, then you may find the duchess is with child, which would defeat the purpose of the murder. To that end, I think we should spread rumors about Sir Gerald here, and the duchess, saying that they are still enamored. You will need to work quickly, Sir Gerald."

"This maid of yours," said Gerald, "she must furnish you with details of the duke's comings and goings."

"Agreed," snapped Lord Werford.

"In that case," said Gerald silkily, "the sight of your money would strengthen my arm greatly."

Lord Werford nodded to Percy, who went over to a bookcase, one of those glass-fronted ones where the books were carefully shrouded by green curtains in case the very sight of literature should put a gentleman off his port. Underneath the books was a cupboard, and out of this cupboard Percy drew a large, thick, black leather wallet.

He rose and dropped the wallet on Gerald's lap. Gerald flipped it open. It was stuffed with notes.

Paper money, he thought ruefully. Gold would have been more satisfactory if he had to leave the country quickly. But with this money, he could buy new clothes and jewels and keep a carriage. He would go to Tattersall's in the morning and bid for a pair of matched bays. He would . . .

He realized that Percy and Lord Werford were eyeing him narrowly. Now was not the time to dream.

"We do not think you should come here again," said Lord Werford. "But you will meet us at Giles's coffeehouse in Cheapside tomorrow at noon; we will have found out by then the duke's movements. Do not fail us."

"I won't fail," said Sir Gerald cheerfully. He could not think of anything much other than the money in the huge wallet on his lap. The rudiments of conscience stirred somewhere within him, but he knew from experience that a good bottle of brandy would soon put paid to any unmanly qualms.

When he returned to his lodgings, it was to find a terse note from Lady Macdonald, demanding that he present himself at her box at the opera.

He wondered whether to ignore it or go and tell her that that particular game was at an end. But after some thought, he realized he needed her help. Alice and the duke must be kept apart at all costs. If Alice became pregnant, it would mean the awful Werford would expect him to murder her as well. And I don't hurt ladies, thought Gerald sanctimoniously as he called for his man to lay out his evening clothes.

When he got there, the opera was ablaze with lights. He sat in the back of Lady Macdonald's box and waited for the interval. Catalini was singing, and apart from reflecting on the fact that the diva received two hundred guineas for each performance and that she was so popular that she was about the only performer who could reduce society to a respectful listening silence, Gerald waited patiently, unmoved by the golden voice from the stage.

Madame Angelica Catalini's voice was first noticed at the early age of twelve when she was in the convent of St. Lucia, at Gubbio, in Italy. At the age of fifteen, due to her father's financial ruin, she was compelled to leave the convent and earn a living on the stage. At the age of sixteen, she made her debut at Venice, in an opera by Nasolini, and afterward sang at Florence, at La Scala in Milan, at Trieste, Rome, and Naples. Her fame got her an engagement in Lisbon, where she married Monsieur Valabregue, a French officer. Finally after Madrid and Paris, she came to London in 1806 and speedily became the rage. She was unwittingly the cause of the Old Price Riots. The theater raised its prices, stating that this was because they also had to pay Mrs. Siddons fifty guineas a performance as well as pay the opera singer's high fees, and that the theater's insurance premium was high, but the mob went wild, forgetting about Mrs. Siddons and blaming Catalini, the foreigner, for the increased prices. The riots went on for months. Their other grievance was that some of the public boxes had been made private. This they said was pandering to the vices of a decadent aristocracy. The riots went on until both sides, the law and the mob, became weary of them.

While Gerald sat in impatient indifference, Catalini sang on to a hushed house, as if she had never been the center of any riot or strife, and the days when the loud voices from the pit calling out, "No foreigners!" were, on this fashionable evening, definitely a thing of the past.

At last the interval came. Lady Macdonald was

not alone. She was accompanied by a tired-looking, middle-aged Scotchwoman, some dusty relative, Gerald correctly surmised, who had been dug out of mothballs to give the dashing widow a spurious air of respectability.

"I want to speak to you in private," he murmured.

Her cold eyes surveyed him. "Take me for a walk," she said, "or we will be interrupted by my courtiers."

They promenaded along the alley at the back of the boxes. "Now," said Lady Macdonald sweetly, "I assume you are here to pay me my money back."

"If you mean the Taylors' ball, that was your scheme and I am not to blame if it did not work," said Gerald. "Why so bitter? Did Ferrant give you your marching orders?"

"Ah, yes, he is become quite the puritan."

"Courage, my beauty. The game is not over."

They fell silent as a couple approached them. Gerald bowed and Lady Macdonald curtsied, and then, as soon as the couple had passed, Gerald said, "If Ferrant believed his little wife to be still enamored of me, you could have him back."

Lady Macdonald looked at him scornfully. "And how do you propose to do that?"

"We gossip, beloved. A little word here, a little sigh there. Now the duchess has a friend in Lucy Vere, who increases daily with child. Women in such a condition are easily prey to fancies. Her husband is a bosom friend of Ferrant. We do not gossip to Mrs. Vere direct, mark you, but discreetly to one of her friends. Mrs. Vere will confide in her husband. *He* might say something to Ferrant."

"The duchess will deny all."

"As she would if she were guilty," he said smoothly.

She tapped his arm with her fan. "You are a wicked man, Sir Gerald, but I confess you have put me in a good humor. Go ahead with your plan. You gossip on your side and I will confide in Mrs. Tumley, who is a friend of Lucy Vere's and a gossipy rattle if ever there was one."

He smiled to himself. Alice, hurt and rejected by her husband, would be all the readier to fall into his arms after the duke's death. He realized with surprise that he was contemplating this murder without a qualm and felt extremely powerful and Machiavellian.

Alice was beginning to feel at ease with her husband for the first time. He laughed at the Irishmen's tall stories and capped them with some of his own. They had a pleasant supper in the Star and Garter at Richmond, sitting in the bay of the window and watching the Thames, silver in the moonlight, flow past.

When it was time to leave, he suggested to Alice that, as he was driving them, she might like to accompany him on the box. Alice was helped up onto the high perch while Mrs. Duggan and the two gallants climbed inside. The duke tenderly wrapped Alice in an enormous bearskin rug despite her protests that the night was fine and warm. The drive home was exhilarating for Alice as they raced through the moonlit countryside. She was very aware of her husband, of his long, white hands on the reins, of the muscled strength of his legs on the spatterboard. She stole little glances at his high, strong profile, and once, when he turned his head and smiled down at her, she felt strangely breathless.

They deposited Mrs. Duggan at her home and then took Lord Dunfear and Mr. Donnelly to their lodgings before going home themselves. Ostlers came running around from the mews to seize the horses' heads. The duke climbed down and then lifted Alice down, holding her briefly in his arms before setting her on the ground.

For the first time they walked up the staircase together until they reached the landing, where their ways divided. Alice turned to go to her own apartments and then turned back and held out her hand.

"Thank you for a wonderful evening, Ferrant," she said shyly.

He took her hand in his. "My name is John," he said.

"Thank you, John."

He turned her hand over and slowly undid the little buttons at the wrist of her glove, then drew off the glove and bent and kissed her wrist. His lips were warm. He then straightened up and looked into her eyes. Her face in the shadowy landing looked young and soft and her eyes enormous.

He placed both his long hands on either side of her face and bent and kissed her, his mouth now firm and hard, pressing down on her soft lips, which trembled under his own.

He sighed against her lips and wound his arms about her and lifted her up against his body. The rigid spasm of fear that had gripped her when he had first begun to kiss her, obscure, half-remembered memories of what men were supposed to do to women flooding her brain, ebbed away. There was nothing threatening in his kisses. She hoped naively he was enjoying himself. It was a bit suffocating, but provided she kept her nose to the side so that she was able to breath, she would be all right. She supposed he would soon carry her off to bed and do whatever it was that gentlemen did that every woman was supposed to grit her teeth and endure, and that would be a great pity, for she was reading a fascinating romance and had promised herself the luxury of a few chapters before falling asleep. Then there was Oracle to pet and talk to. He released her lips and set her down and stood back a little, surveying her. Alice felt sure she should say something or other, but she felt very embarrassed. She shuffled her feet and looked at the floor.

He put one long finger under her chin and tilted her face up. "Go to bed, Alice," he said quietly. "I' faith, you are very young."

Alice bobbed a quick curtsy and escaped to her own quarters. She had told Betty not to wait up for her and so, as she got ready for bed, she chatted to Oracle about the evening in Richmond; the bird replied with squawks as it hopped about the room, glad of this temporary freedom from its cage.

Alice got into bed and reached for the romance she had been reading. She read on until the hero rescued the heroine from the dungeon of an Italian castle. He clasped her in his arms and kissed her, and she swooned with emotion. Alice put down the book with a little frown. Perhaps Ferrant had expected *her* to swoon. What of all that tremulous love she had felt for Sir Gerald? But when she had thought of him and being married to him, she had thought how jolly it would be when they set up house together. Gerald had never kissed her. He had been about to when the duke had come upon them in the rose garden. The duke smelled of clean starched linen and lavender water. Gerald had smelled of brandy, sweat, and tobacco.

If only she had not been so frightened, she was sure she would have enjoyed his kisses. He should have tried harder and longer. He was disappointed in her. He had said she was very young. Perhaps she should have shown more sensibility. But ladies were never supposed to show any passion whatsoever, only sluts did that, or so Alice had been told by parents and governess alike. But it was surely very ungenerous to be kissed without some answering show of affection. Alice wrinkled her brow. She would need to instigate the next kiss, and that would make things even.

She had half forgotten this resolve when she went down for breakfast. She never breakfasted in her room, always preferring to be up and downstairs at an hour that society would consider sadly unfashionable.

She was startled to find her husband in the breakfast room and nearly stammered out an apology and retreated before she remembered that they were supposed to be on good terms. Then she remembered her resolve to kiss him. It was difficult to see how she could manage it because after a murmured, "Good morning," the duke had sat down at the table and barricaded himself behind the *Morning Post*.

Alice helped herself to tea and toast, thinking that the sooner she kissed him and got it over with, the sooner she could feel easy in her conscience. But she could not kiss him through a newspaper. He was in riding dress while she was in her undress—wrapper, lacy nightgown, and frilly nightcap—and she felt at a sartorial disadvantage.

"Ferrant," she ventured.

"I told you to call me John," came a voice from behind the newspaper.

"I have something on my conscience . . . John."

He put down his newspaper and watched her, his eyes guarded. She was looking exceptionally beautiful with her auburn hair cascading down her back and with her thick-fringed hazel eyes regarding him so seriously.

"I suggest you unburden yourself," said the duke politely.

"I feel when you kissed me last night that I was lacking some necessary warmth," said Alice.

"You were, indeed," he said amiably. "But such things cannot be forced."

"The willingness was there," she said seriously. "I am not practiced, you see. I was reading this amazing book, and when the hero kisses the heroine, she swoons from an excess of emotion."

"The sad fact is that I do not wish you to manufacture feelings you do not have," said the duke.

"I think it is nerves," said Alice firmly. "Yes, that must be the case. For we have been enemies and now we are suddenly friends, you see, and so my feelings perhaps have not caught up with the new circumstances of our relationship."

His eyes flashed with amusement. "Do you plan to do anything to alter your feelings?"

"Oh, yes, for that would only be fair. I really think I ought to kiss you, Ferrant . . . I mean, John."

"Had you any particular occasion in mind?"

"Perhaps now would be a good idea . . . and then I could get finished with it and feel comfortable. The servants do not trouble one at breakfast."

His eyes mocked her. "I am on this side of the table, my heart, and you are on the other."

"Well, then," she said bravely, "I shall rise and come to you, John, if you will take the trouble to stand."

The duke dutifully stood up.

She walked round and looked up at him towering over her. Then she turned and stooped and picked up a footstool, placed it between them, and stood on it. "Now what?" he asked, his eyes dancing.

"If you would please close your eyes, I would not feel so self-conscious."

He closed his eyes.

She put her little hands on either side of his face, copying his actions of the night before, and pressed her mouth to his. Good heavens, he thought, half-exasperated, half-amused, I swear the minx is timing this kiss so that it is exactly the same as I gave her. He slid his hand under the heavy masses of her hair and caressed the back of her neck. Alice began to sense a warm, drugged feeling coursing through her body. Perhaps she should put her arms around him. And then she forgot about everything but that mouth now pressing hard and searching on her own. Everything became sensation and sweetness and longing.

The door opened and Hoskins, the butler, walked in. The couple broke apart. Hoskins quickly withdrew.

Alice stared up at the duke in a drowned way. Now, he thought, now I should scoop her up in my arms and take her to bed. There came a scratching at the door. "What is it?" called the duke angrily.

"Mr. Vere is called," came the butler's voice.

"Damn. Edward. I had forgot. I promised to go riding with Edward."

"Then you must go," said Alice, stepping down from the footstool.

"But later we shall go for a drive in the Park. Are you free?"

"Oh, yes," said Alice happily, not knowing what she was engaged to do that day but meaning to cancel everything.

He smiled and gave her a sudden last hard kiss on the mouth.

He and Edward rode easily under the trees on Rotten Row. Edward was wondering how to bring up the matter his wife had commanded him to interrogate the duke about. It had all happened at the ball after the opera the night before. Mrs. Tumley, a chattering matron, had sought out Lucy and the two had become engaged in conversation. On the road home, Lucy, in anguish, had told him that, according to Mrs. Tumley, Alice was setting out on an affair with Sir Gerald, had been meeting him in secret, while the duke intended to get a speedy divorce and marry Lady Macdonald.

When at last they reined in, Edward said cautiously, "How is Alice?"

"Blooming, my dear Edward."

"Never asked you before," said Edward awkwardly, "but I feel things got off to a bad start with that cursed bird at the wedding."

The duke looked at him shrewdly. "What's this all about, Edward?"

"Nasty gossips are plaguing my Lucy with the intelligence that Alice is enamored of Sir Gerald and has been seen with him and—"

The duke spurred his horse and set off like the wind. Cursing, Edward followed, not catching up with the duke until the far side of the Park. The duke reined in and patted his horse's neck. "Never again, Edward," he said evenly, "relate any gossip about me or my wife to me again. Is that understood?"

"Of course, of course," said Edward hurriedly. "Dashed sorry. It's Lucy's condition. Everything upsets her."

Chapter Six

ALICE PASSED THE TIME, waiting for her husband to arrive to take her driving in the Park, by reading a magazine. In it a writer had satirized the diary of a woman of fashion that led Alice to think that she herself led a remarkably staid life.

Dreamed of the captain—certainly a fine man—counted my card money—lost considerably—never play again with the dowager—breakfasted at *two* ... dined at seven at Lady Rackett's—the captain there—more than usually agreeable—went to the opera—captain in the party—house prodigiously crowded—my *ci devant* husband in the opposite box—rather *mal à-propos*—but no matter—*telles choses sont*—look into Lady Squander's rout—positively a mob—sat down to cards—in great luck—won a cool hundred of my Lord Lackwit, and fifty of the baron—returned home at five in the morning—indulged in half an hour's reflection—resolved on reformation, and erased my name from the Picnic Society.

Alice laughed at the last line of this satire. The Picnic Club was that most reputable of institutions, engaged as it was in musical performances and amateur theatricals. The lady of society had chosen the most respectable of interests to forego in the name of reformation.

Her husband walked into the room and she ran to him, laughing, and showed him the article. "Correct in every detail," he said sourly, glancing through it, "down to the bad French. If society women insist on larding their conversation with French, why cannot they at least learn to speak it properly?"

"*Tish!* It is not just Englishwomen but Englishmen who are deficient in that respect," said Alice. "Englishmen who go on the Grand Tour are well versed in Ancient Greek and Latin but not in any of the languages of the countries they must pass through. They leave all knowledge of foreign languages to their couriers."

"Ah, yes, Sir Gerald Warby has been on the Grand Tour, I believe," said the duke.

Alice blushed fiery red in anger and embarrassment. She thought all that nonsense had been resolved. But the duke saw that blush and put it down to guilt. He had never been jealous before and wondered why he could hardly control his own sour anger. From upstairs came banging and clanging as the decorators continued their work on the drawing room. He had a sudden urge to say that he liked his house as it was and would she please leave it alone, but the pettiness of that thought brought him somewhat to his senses.

Why should he listen to gossip—whether relayed to him by Edward or anyone else? He smiled suddenly at Alice. "Fetch your bonnet and pelisse, my dear, and we will take the air."

Relieved by his abrupt change of humor, Alice

ran to put on a pretty Lavinia bonnet and a pere-line, instead of a pelisse, that short cape of fine muslin trimmed with bugle beads that was more of an ornament than a protection against the weather. Men were indeed odd. Mama had warned her that they were subject to a Disorder of the Spleen from time to time, which made the creatures tetchy.

And his evident good humor lasted as he drove her competently to the Park in a smart phaeton. Alice began to relax and enjoy herself. Her es-trangement from her husband had caused her a cer-tain amount of social isolation. Now all could see they were on the best of terms.

Soldiers were drilling at the far side of the Park, a military display rather than the military neces-sity it had been during the wars with the French.

They bowled along, the duke nodding to people he knew. Alice felt very proud to be seen out with him. He smiled down at her. "Had enough of the quizzes?" he asked.

"Let's go round one more time," said Alice. "I want everyone to see us together. And I want a closer look at the soldiers."

"How unfashionable of you," he mocked, to dis-guise the fact that he was highly pleased. "The fashionables are thinning out now."

The carriage moved slowly under the trees. They had just come abreast a stand of bushes quite near where the soldiers were drilling. The front rank of soldiers raised their muskets and fired a volley in the air, making Alice start, and the carriage rug slipped from her knees. Holding the reins in one hand, the duke stooped to raise the rug round her knees again and, as he bent down, there was a sharp report. "Those soldiers," said Alice. "What a waste of ammunition."

The duke reined in his team and then slowly removed his curly-brimmed beaver and held it out. "Why!" exclaimed Alice, "There is a hole in your good hat . . ." Her voice trailed away and she looked at him in horror.

"Exactly," he said grimly. He called to his tiger on the backstrap to go to the horse's heads and then he jumped down. "I won't be long," he said. "I am just going to have a word with the colonel in charge of those men."

Alice sat looking about her. What a terrible thing to have happened. Sometimes it seemed as if there were guns going off all over London—from military displays to Cockney sportsmen who brought their guns into town and fired at dogs and cats and geese. And then a movement to her right caught her eye. Walking briskly away, near the stand of bushes, was a figure that looked familiar. She leaned a little forward. Surely she recognized that long body and those short legs. Surely that was Sir Gerald. She felt suddenly cold. Could he . . . would he dare . . . fire at her husband? But the idea was preposterous.

"I am going for a little walk," she called to the tiger.

She jumped nimbly down and forced herself to walk slowly round to the back of the stand of bushes until she found herself screened from the tiger.

Then she parted the branches and peered into the green undergrowth. A musket, a military musket, was lying on the ground. Then she heard her husband's voice asking where she was and hurried back.

"The colonel says it could not have been any of his men. He watched them and they all fired in the air," said the duke.

"John, I am afraid someone *was* firing at you," said Alice. "There is a musket hidden in those bushes and I think the shot might have come from there."

His face grim, he went to look, drawing the musket out of its hiding place and sniffing the barrel. "Recently fired," he said. "Did you see anyone?"

Alice shook her head. It could not have been Sir Gerald. Her eyes must have been playing her tricks. It was probably one of the Cockney sportsmen firing at a bird in a tree and hitting the duke's hat by mistake. To mention Sir Gerald's name would start up all the old scandal. But as soon as she had shaken her head, she immediately wished she had told him the truth. To tell him now would seem as if her first impulse had been to shield Sir Gerald, and she could not have him believe that. She looked wretched, but the duke put it down to fright.

He walked back and stopped a smart carriage. Mrs. Tumley's rouged face looked at him in surprise. "Please, would you take my wife home," said the duke. "I have an urgent matter to attend to here."

"Gladly," said Mrs. Tumley, goggling with curiosity as Alice was helped in beside her.

"What was all that about?" asked Mrs. Tumley as they drove off.

"Someone shot at my husband and would have killed him had he not been bending down at the time," said Alice.

"How frightful!" shrieked Mrs. Tumley. "My dear

duchess, I feel quite faint. There are murderers and assassins everywhere."

"I think it might prove to be some Cockney sportsman," said Alice quietly, wishing she could get that retreating figure—looking *so* like Sir Gerald Warby—out of her head.

"You must be all of a quiver, but then you are used to living dangerously," said Mrs. Tumley, with a titter.

"What do you mean by that remark?"

"Oh, my dear," Mrs. Tumley put a gloved hand on Alice's knee. She glanced around and lowered her voice. "We all know you are pining for Sir Gerald."

"How dare you!" said Alice furiously. "How dare you spread such malicious gossip? It is not true. Coachman! Stop here!"

Alice jumped down from the carriage and walked off along Park Street, her face flaming.

So it's true after all, thought Mrs. Tumley with satisfaction. She would not have been so vehement in her denial if there had been nothing in it. So instead of driving on, she went to call on a Mrs. Grange, and among Mrs. Grange's callers was Lucy Vere, who listened, appalled, to the gossip.

She declared it was all lies and promptly took her leave. The ladies nodded wisely after she had gone. Lucy Vere was a friend of the duchess's. Of course she would try to defend her friend. And so gossip, fueled by envy of the pretty duchess, continued to spread.

Lucy went home, sat down at her desk, and wrote a note to Sir Gerald requesting him to call. She knew Edward was not expected back for another two hours. Then she waited impatiently.

Sir Gerald arrived quite promptly. He had been in his lodgings, cursing himself for his failed attempt on the duke's life. He was feeling sick and shaky. He felt he could not make another attempt. It was one thing to dream about taking a man's life, another thing to actually try to do it. The summons from Lucy intrigued him. Perhaps Alice had sent him a message through Lucy. If only he had never accepted that money from her parents to go away. He could have married the girl and had her fortune.

Lucy received him in the library of her home, a setting she felt more suited to grave business than the drawing room, despite the fact that the library contained only one bookshelf full of romances. Edward did not read anything other than the morning papers.

"Be seated, Sir Gerald," said Lucy. "I have something very important to discuss with you."

He sat down. Lucy regarded him steadily. She had always thought him a handsome man and had envied Alice in the days before she, Lucy, had met her darling Edward. There was some change in Sir Gerald, she thought, a certain loss of innocence. There were dark shadows under his black eyes and his mouth had become fuller.

"I heard some very distressing gossip this afternoon," said Lucy.

Gerald sat very still. Surely he could not be suspected of that attempt on Ferrant's life. He had first established an alibi by riding to a curricle race at Hammersmith. As soon as he had talked to as many people as possible, he had slipped away and ridden as hard as he could back to London. He was sure no one had seen him in the Park. He had heard that the duke was to take Alice driving and he knew of the military exercise. He had purchased an army musket and had carried it to the Park. He had hid in the stand of bushes, hoping that the duke and Alice might drive over to look at the soldiers. That they should have driven past just after that volley of shots was a remarkable piece of luck—but the duke *would* choose that moment to stoop in the carriage—and so the musket ball had gone harmlessly through his hat.

"Mrs. Tumley," said Lucy, "is spreading gossip about you and Alice."

"Fie for shame," said Gerald, with relief. "Alice is lost to me." His agile brain was working. No use telling this friend of Alice's any lies about a liaison. On the other hand, she could be put to use.

"I know there is no truth in it," said Lucy, "and I want you to tell everyone so."

"My dear Mrs. Vere," he said, putting his hand on his heart, "your wish is my command."

"Yes . . . well, very fine, to be sure," said Lucy uneasily.

"But there is one thing you do not realize, Mrs. Vere. I have been much wronged. Alice's parents called on me and told me to leave Alice alone . . . begged me. They said she was in love with Ferrant and had not the courage to tell me. Ah, the pain and humiliation of it all. My heart nigh broke."

"Very sad," said Lucy uncomfortably. "But that is all past and she is married, and so . . ."

"And so I must accept it. But she is so unhappy. Surely you have noticed that. This . . . er . . . flaunting of Lady Macdonald . . ."

A shadow crossed Lucy's face. "Let us not talk about that."

"As you will. What concerns me is that I have not had a proper chance to explain myself to Alice. All I want is one meeting."

"That would not be wise. You know the way of the world, sir. A man may have mistresses, but a woman must never cause any scandal whatsoever."

"But it is only one meeting, I beg of you. If you could prevail on Alice to see me, just once. I could also tell her about these dreadful rumors, and together we could scotch them."

Lucy looked at him doubtfully. "To be frank, if there are any embers of warmth toward you left, Sir Gerald, I do not feel like doing anything to fan them."

"You would not. A final good-bye would be to everyone's advantage."

"Very well. I will call on Alice tomorrow and see what I can do."

Gerald stood up to take his leave. Just to be on the safe side, he should establish that alibi even more. "I had the pleasure of meeting your husband this afternoon, a curricle race at Hammersmith," he said as he bowed his way out.

He felt pleased. The intrigue had bolstered his spirits. "Hey, Warby!" cried Mr. Jermyn, a Bond Street lounger. "What news?"

Gerald looked at him solemnly. "There is no truth in the rumors that I am having an affair with the Duchess of Ferrant," he said. "Tell everyone."

Mr. Jermyn goggled at him. "Oh, I will, I will," he said, and then went on to his club, where he regaled his cronies with the fact that the Duchess of Ferrant was having an affair with Sir Gerald Warby—and Sir Gerald was trying to cover up the fact in the clumsiest way possible, which is exactly what Sir Gerald had guessed he would do.

Alice was dismayed to receive a message from her husband saying that he would not be home until late. The duke was continuing his questioning of the soldiers and anyone else who had happened to be in the Park at the time. One soldier, brighter than the rest, had vouchsafed that he had seen a fellow walking away from the bushes with an empty canvas gun bag. No, the soldier had said, he had not remarked on him particularly. Had thought idly that he was one of those Cockneys come to see the drill. He described the man as being tall and wearing a wideawake on his head, but couldn't remember much else.

Mrs. Duggan called to remind Alice that they were engaged to go to Lady Markman's picnic on the morrow if the weather held fine. After she had left, Alice was sitting flipping through a pile of invitation cards, discussing with Oracle whether she should go to one of the social events on her own, when Lucy was announced. Lucy had decided she could not bear to wait until tomorrow. Edward had not come home. He had sent a note to say he would join her at the opera later.

Alice embraced her warmly. "I am so glad to see you, Lucy. Such a frightful thing has happened. Someone shot at Ferrant in the Park."

"Merciful heavens," said Lucy. "You must have had a dreadful shock. Have they found who did it?"

Alice shook her head. "Ferrant is still making inquiries." She suddenly wanted to unburden herself, to tell Lucy about that man she had seen, that man who had looked so like Sir Gerald, but Lucy had begun to speak again.

"I had a visit from Sir Gerald Warby, Alice."

Alice blushed. Lucy said evenly, "This followed a distressing call on Mrs. Grange. Mrs. Tumley was there . . . and she was spreading gossip that you are having an affair with Warby."

"This is awful!"

"Exactly. So I took the liberty of sending for Sir Gerald and telling him to scotch the rumors."

"When was this?" asked Alice.

"Late this afternoon. I was lucky to find him at home. He had just returned from a curricle race in Hammersmith."

Alice felt limp with relief. So it could not have been Sir Gerald in the Park. She had been right to keep her suspicions to herself.

"Sir Gerald quite moved me," Lucy went on, "by the way he described how your parents had coerced him into leaving you. He said they had told him you were in love with Ferrant."

"I shall never forgive them for that," said Alice.

Lucy looked at her sadly. "If you won't forgive them for stopping your marriage to Sir Gerald, surely that means you still long for him."

"No, no," said Alice wretchedly. "I am furious because my parents did not confide in me, because they tricked me."

"Sir Gerald begged me to see you. He wishes to talk to you for one last time, to explain."

"He has already explained," said Alice wearily.

"I suppose I feel a certain sympathy for him," said Lucy earnestly. "He was tricked as well. Could you not spare him a few moments of your time?"

Alice bit her lip. "I cannot have him call here.

But, yes, I think I would like to see him. Perhaps I could beg him to leave London so there would be a chance of all those horrible rumors dying down. I am to go with Mrs. Duggan to Lady Markman's picnic tomorrow. I do not know if Sir Gerald has been invited, but at these hurly-burly affairs an odd uninvited member of society is not remarked on. It is at three in the afternoon in the Surrey fields. Tell him to be there and I can talk to him for a little."

"Everyone will see you together," pointed out Lucy doubtfully. "Can you not meet him in private?"

Alice shook her head. "If anyone saw a private meeting, that would be worse."

"But to return to this shooting," said Lucy. "Who could have possibly done such a thing?"

"I found a musket lying in the bushes," said Alice. "Perhaps one of the soldiers— It was a military musket."

"The Cockney youths often use old army muskets as well for their sport. I don't mean one of them would consider shooting Ferrant as sport. What I mean is that they drink so much, and as soon as they are drunk, all they want to do is shoot things. One of them shot Lady Markman's pug when it had run away from her carriage. And the fellow had the gall to say he thought it was a rat!"

Alice began to feel quite lighthearted. It did not cross her mind that her husband's assailant might have chosen an army musket in the very hope that the soldiers would have been blamed, or some lout from the East End of the City who could afford only an old army weapon.

"I feel it is definitely time to start afresh, Lucy," she said. "Once I have spoken to Sir Gerald and heard what he has to say, then I feel I can begin a new chapter."

Lucy looked at her seriously. "I hope your husband means to start a new chapter as well."

"He has told me about Lady Macdonald. It was a flirtation, Lucy, not an affair, and it is at an end."

Lucy gave Alice an impulsive hug. "You are going to be the most happily married lady in London, and won't *that* confound the gossips!"

Sir Gerald received a letter from Lucy that was waiting for him when he had returned home. He felt exhausted. It had been a long day. First the meeting in the City with Lord Werford and Percy, the discussion with them of the best way to shoot the duke, the getting of the musket, the dash to Hammersmith, the dash back from Hammersmith to the Park, the circuitous approach to that stand of bushes, walking neither too fast nor too slow, his hat pulled down over his eyes to cover his face, and then the failure. He had tracked Werford and Percy down to a coffeehouse in Pall Mall in the evening, and, to their complaints, he had replied waspishly that the whole project of shooting the duke in broad daylight in the Park had been insanity. In future, they would have to trust him and let him do his own planning, to which Lord Werford had barked, "Don't take too long about it," and his eyes had been full of threat.

He scanned Lucy's note and then smiled. It was also his job to see that the duke and Alice did not become close—or the next thing would be that Alice would be with child and Werford would be demanding *her* murder.

He wearily put on his evening clothes and went

out again to search for Lady Macdonald. He was quite prepared to attend every social function in London to find her, but he fortunately called at her home first—and to his relief found her there.

He told her about his planned meeting with Alice at the picnic. "Good," said Lady Macdonald, "but what will you do if Ferrant is there?"

"I do not think he will be," said Gerald. "If she is prepared to speak to me, then she will not want her husband to be witness to it."

Lady Macdonald smiled. "It would be in my interest to get him there. I have been invited."

Gerald thought quickly. All sorts of opportunities at a picnic. Shooting had been clumsy. Now poison was easily available, and poison was subtle. There was arsenic all over London: arsenic in the wallpaper paste to keep down bugs, arsenic in the kitchens to keep down rats, and arsenic used as a cosmetic to clear the skin. Of course, there would be an outcry to see who had killed the great duke. First suspect would be Alice, but he could testify to her innocence and cleverly throw the blame on Lady Macdonald, saying she was mad with jealousy.

"I think perhaps I will send Ferrant a note begging him to meet me there in the name of friendship," said Lady Macdonald. "If his wife tells him she is to go, then he might reply that tomorrow is not a good moment. But if she plans to talk to *you*, then she may lie to him."

Gerald affected a gaiety he did not feel as he asked the all-important question. "What is Ferrant's favorite food? I only ask because the way to a man's heart is through his stomach."

"I will take him some pâté de foie gras," said Lady Macdonald. "He is inordinately fond of that, and I doubt if Lady Markman will have any. Although the wars are over, it is still very expensive and very hard to find."

Gerald left praying that Alice and the duke would not arrive together. If they did, then it meant that Alice had told her husband openly that she wanted a few words with him, Gerald.

Alice did not see her husband at breakfast. The duke had gone out early to fight a duel. He had called at his club late the previous evening and had overheard a young buck telling his friend that the Duchess of Ferrant was having an affair with Sir Gerald Warby. The duke had promptly demanded satisfaction for the insult. Seconds were named. The duel took place at dawn. The young buck missed the duke by a yard, but the duke put a ball into his arm, saw that the surgeon was attending to the young man, and then told him that if he or any of his fellows mentioned such a slur again, he would take him to court. . . . And that, the duke thought ruefully as he tumbled into bed, was what he should have done in the first place, society being more terrified of the law courts than they were of duels.

He rose and dressed and then read the letter from Lady Macdonald. He called his secretary. "Where is the duchess?" he asked.

"Her Grace left a few moments ago with Mrs. Duggan, Lord Dunfear, and Mr. Donnelly."

"Do you know where they have gone?"

"No, Your Grace, but I overheard Mrs. Duggan say that it was a beautiful day for a drive."

The duke frowned down at the letter in his hand. He had treated Lady Macdonald badly. He should have made it clear to her from the beginning that he had no intention of divorcing his wife. But then at that time, he *had* thought of divorcing Alîce. He thought of Alice's sweet kisses and smiled, and felt suddenly in charity with all the world. Yes, he would see Lady Macdonald and be kind and courteous to her—but in a way that would make it plain to everyone that they were friends, nothing more.

To Lady Macdonald's surprise, Gerald called on her the next day and said he was prepared to escort her to the picnic. She regarded him impatiently. "I am not ready yet," she said, "and besides, I do not want to upset Ferrant by turning up with you. Off with you."

But Gerald had found out what he wanted, the reason why he had called. On the table in Lady Macdonald's drawing room stood a jar of foie gras, waxed and sealed. He made a mental note of the brand, Janvier et Fils, bowed and took his leave, and scoured the shops until he had purchased, at great expense, a jar of the same kind. He took it back to his lodgings and with a heated knife carefully removed the wax seals, lifted the lid and mixed in a quantity of arsenic, smoothed the top of the pâté, replaced the lid, and resealed it. Then he hired a curricle and drove briskly in the direction of the Surrey fields, feeling again that surge of power.

When he arrived, he noticed that Alice was there with Mrs. Duggan and those two Irishmen, and also noticed with pleasure—from Mrs. Duggan's startled look—that Alice had told her nothing about his going to be there. He smiled blandly on Lady Markman, who was saying loudly and acidly that she could not remember inviting him, and then went and mingled with the guests. He chatted and laughed with people he knew, but out of the corner of his eye, he watched the arriving carriages.

He was rewarded by the sight of Lady Macdonald, driving herself in a smart phaeton, her maid beside her clutching that jar of pâté. Lady Macdonald and the maid descended; the pâté was left on the carriage seat. Quickly Gerald went to his own carriage and retrieved his own pot of pâté, and effected the switch when the footmen, grooms, and coachmen were busy gossiping.

Then he returned to the picnic. People were lying on rugs on the grass or strolling about. He approached Alice and bowed low. "Would you do me the honor of walking with me for a little, Duchess?"

Mrs. Duggan put a hand on Alice's arm, but Alice rose to her feet and said quietly, "Only for a little. I shall not be long, Mrs. Duggan."

Timing! Oh, what perfect timing, thought Lady Macdonald as the Duke of Ferrant drove up.

She fluttered over to him, her filmy muslin skirts blowing about her body in the light breeze. "Ferrant!" she cried gaily. "So you are come after all."

"I had not time to reply to your letter," he said, bowing over her hand. Then his eyes went past her to the squat figure of Mrs. Duggan, seated on the grass with Donnelly and Dunfear.

He frowned. "Is my wife here?" he asked.

"Yes," said Lady Macdonald, letting an embarrassed look appear in her eyes. "Er ... I suppose she is somewhere."

Only a moment before, thought the duke bleakly, the day had been full of light and color. Now the picnic was a strangely gray scene, and at the edge of that gray scene walked his wife—on the arm of Sir Gerald Warby.

Alice did not spend long with Sir Gerald. She listened gravely to his protestations of undying love and his repeated apologies for having sent her that letter. Then she said earnestly that he could best please her by leaving London and putting an end to the rumors. Up until then, Alice had been feeling sorry for him, and guilty at the same time, for she had been secretly wondering why she had ever thought herself in love with him. But when, in what she thought was a rather stagy manner, he put his hand on his heart and said that to be in her neighborhood was all he asked of life and he could not dream of leaving London while she was in it, she felt herself feeling trapped and irritated and said brusquely, "It is time I returned to my friends. I have granted you this time, Sir Gerald, but it must not happen again."

And as she walked back to the picnic, she almost stopped dead at the scene before her eyes. Her husband was sprawled on a pile of cushions next to Lady Macdonald and was smiling up into her eyes. The day was warm or, thought Alice waspishly, Lady Macdonald might have died of exposure, her gown was so thin.

Feeling small and dingy, Alice sank down beside Mrs. Duggan.

"What were you after doing a thing like that for?" demanded Mrs. Duggan. "Faith, that husband of yours arrived just in time to see yourself promenading with Sir Gerald. And if you wonder why he is flirting with that trollop, you have only yourself to blame."

Alice watched miserably. A Highland servant of

Lady Macdonald's was crouched over a spirit stove making toast and looking as if he thought the whole business beneath him. The maid fetched the jar of pâté. The duke looked delighted. Lady Macdonald took a slice of toast from the Highlander and spread pâté on it, then held it, laughing, up to the duke's mouth.

But at the same time, a scabby cur ran up, a mangy half-dead creature. With a muttered curse, the Highlander went forward to boot it away, but the duke laughed and held out the toast covered in pâté to the animal, who gulped it down. Alice saw Lady Macdonald pout prettily and say something, saw the duke laugh again as he covered another piece of toast with pâté and give it to the dog.

And then the poor animal began to shiver and shake and roll its eyes. Convulsions tore at its thin body. It was dreadfully sick and stretched its length on the grass, its eyes closed. Sir Gerald had laced the pâté with enough arsenic to fell an ox.

There was a startled silence. For everyone had seen what had happened, everyone's eyes traveling avidly from Alice's face to her husband's.

"I really don't think we should eat this," said the duke. "The animal was on its last legs, but still . . ."

Servants had built a large bonfire at the edge of the picnic field. Sir Gerald sped up and seized the jar of pâté. "I wouldn't trust anything that comes out of France," he cried. "Let's burn this nasty stuff."

Alice, very still, watched as he walked through a cheering crowd and hurled the jar of pâté into the center of the bonfire. Servants carried the dog to the edge of the field and threw it down. She shivered. Something was badly wrong. She could not explain it.

The duke noticed her white, set face. He said quickly to Lady Macdonald, "I am behaving disgracefully, you know, giving the gossips fuel by staying here with you. I beg your pardon."

Mrs. Duggan saw him striding toward them and said to Donnelly and Dunfear, "Up with you, lazybones, and let us go and get some champagne."

"I can call a servant," said Lord Dunfear lazily, and then yelped with pain as Mrs. Duggan pinched his arm.

They left as the duke arrived.

He sat down next to Alice. She bent her head, the wide brim of her Lavinia hat shading her face.

He was about to berate her for talking to Sir Gerald, for having *dared* to talk to Sir Gerald, but as soon as he opened his mouth, he considered his own behavior. *She* had merely walked and talked with Sir Gerald who was, after all, an old friend. She had not flirted with him or smiled on him. So instead, he said, "You overset me. I arrived in time to see you walking with Warby. I have already had to threaten gossips who are circulating a tale that you and Warby are having an affair."

"Lucy came to see me," said Alice in a low voice. "She had heard the rumors, too, and had sent for Sir Gerald to say they must be scotched. He begged her to see me. He wanted to talk to me for one last time. He—he said my parents had called on him and lied to him, saying I was in love with you. That was the reason he went away. All he wanted to do was explain and say good-bye."

The duke sighed, threw his hat on the grass, and ran his hands through his thick hair.

"Why do you think I flirted with Lady Macdonald? I asked my secretary where you had gone and he was under the impression that you had simply gone for a drive with your friends. Lady Macdonald had written to me, asking to see me for old times' sake. It has been a misunderstanding. I must believe you, and you must believe me." He wanted to take her hand and draw her to him, but that phrase of hers—that her parents had told Sir Gerald that she was in love with him, with all its implications that she had *not* been in love with him at all—hurt him dreadfully. She had kissed him dutifully because she was trying to be a good wife. They would need to put these scandals behind them and try to get to know each other.

"We must start again," he said. "We are still strangers to each other, are we not?"

"Yes," whispered Alice.

A tear rolled down her nose and plopped on her dress.

"No, don't cry," he said quickly. "You make me feel like an angry father rather than a husband. Let us walk together and look as affectionate as we can manage to try to repair some of the damage we have done."

He helped Alice to her feet and they walked off together. He began to ask her about the changes to the drawing room; Alice answered shyly at first and then in a more relaxed manner. It would be all finished in a week's time, she said, and he must not look at it until then. It was to be a surprise.

They reached the corner of the field and Alice stepped back with a cry, for the dead dog lay in front of them. "Don't look at it," he said. "I shall send some of Lady Markman's servants to bury the creature. Well, we shall never know what killed the animal, for Warby threw the whole pot of stuff into the fire."

"I wish he had not," said Alice, "for we could have taken it to an apothecary and gotten him to look for poison."

The duke laughed. "My mad behavior has really overset you. That poor dog was near death and had probably been eating all sorts of rubbish."

"Of course," said Alice, looking relieved. "Oh, here is Lucy with Edward."

The Veres joined them. The duke asked Lucy how she was feeling and walked with her while Edward fell into step beside Alice.

"I gather you were at a curricle race at Hammersmith yesterday," said Alice.

"Yes, and lost a packet of money, but don't tell Lucy that. I feel such a fool."

Something prompted Alice to say, "I believe Sir Gerald was there."

"Hey, what? Oh, yes, him," said Edward, with a scowl. "Fact is, Alice, he's not very good ton and can't take a snub. Ran around bowing and scraping and talking to people who would rather not know him. And then right at the start of the race, he rode off hell-for-leather."

Alice felt a lurch of fear. "I wonder why he did not stay to watch," she said.

"Demme, who knows or cares? Probably off to shoot something. Had a ratty canvas gun bag with him."

Chapter Seven

ALICE FELT VERY COLD. Everything looked suddenly threatening. There was no sign of Sir Gerald. Even Lady Macdonald was walking toward her carriage. There had been that pâté, thrown so conveniently in the fire. But such things did not happen outside the pages of romances. Had Gerald appeared mad with thwarted passion? No, there had been something stagy about him. But the Gerald she had known, the Gerald she had been looking forward to marrying, would never have hurt a fly. She should voice her suspicions of Gerald to her husband and let him handle it. But what if she were wrong? The scandal! The hurt to Gerald! It did not bear thinking of. But why had he left that curricle race carrying a gun bag, a canvas gun bag? The man she had seen near those bushes had been carrying an empty canvas gun bag!

She would need to wait and watch and pray that nothing else happened. Gerald had, in his way, been wronged by her parents. If only he would go away!

Lucy came up to her. "What is the matter, Alice? You are looking quite pale."

Alice forced a smile. "A harrowing afternoon, Lucy. I did not expect Ferrant to be here, and neither did he expect to see me. It is like one of those comedies at the Haymarket—or would be if one were not involved in it oneself. But Ferrant and I have resolved our differences."

Lucy looked relieved. "Oh, I would give anything to see you as happy as I." She looked cautiously over her shoulder. Edward had dropped back to talk to the duke, exchanging places with his wife. Both men were deep in conversation. She whispered to Alice, "Sad as it all has been, would you not say that your parents did you a favor? I never knew Sir Gerald really well, but he has changed I think."

Again Alice experienced that stab of dread. "We all change as we grow," she said. "Gerald was left only that small estate and the house when his parents died. He is a brave man. He was knighted when he was only twenty!"

"I remember the excitement of that," said Lucy. "His Majesty was traveling through the county and his horses ran away with the carriage, and it was Gerald who rode to the horses' heads and subdued them. He was such a hero to us all. Do you remember, Alice? When we knew he was going to be in the village, we would all find some excuse to be there as well so as just to look at him."

And Alice remembered, standing with her governess and looking in awe at the young man who had been knighted by the king. How brave and noble he had seemed, the very stuff of romance.

Then her first ball, and Gerald asking her to dance, and how she had felt the world had not more joy to offer. Life had seemed so innocent and simple then. She loved Gerald and would marry him, and they would live happily ever after. Her father's mutterings that Gerald had done nothing to improve the poor condition of his estate went unheeded by Alice.

To add to Alice's bewildered thoughts as she walked along beside Lucy was the nagging fear that her husband might not be so disinterested in Lady Macdonald as he claimed to be. How neatly he had explained away his flirting.

They were joined by Mrs. Duggan, Mr. Donnelly, and Lord Dunfear. "Is everything well?" asked Mrs. Duggan, her small periwinkle eyes searching Alice's face.

"Oh, yes," said Alice.

"You haven't eaten anything," said Mrs. Duggan.

"I do not feel very hungry." Alice looked about her and shivered. "Besides, the sun has gone in."

The duke came up to her. "We'll go home," he said. "You may have an hour's rest before we go out this evening."

"Where are we going?"

"Alas! A duty supper party at Lord Werford's. We need not trouble about the nasty old man after this one event."

Gerald found Lord Werford and Percy waiting for him at his rooms and scowled horribly. "I thought the whole idea was that I was not to be associated with you," he said, flinging himself into an armchair.

"Extreme measures," barked Lord Werford. "So far you have not been successful. Now we are going to try our hand, and if we succeed, you may hand back that advance we gave you."

Gerald eyed them narrowly. If they succeeded,

then they would not hesitate to kill *him*, for he could always blackmail them, and he was sure they had thought of that.

"How do you plan to do it?" he demanded scornfully.

"Ferrant and his duchess are coming to supper tonight. Turtle soup. Shake of arsenic and the deed is done."

"And how do you get the arsenic into the soup without your servants knowing about it?"

"I keep old-fashioned ways," said Lord Werford. "Serve from the head of the table. Plates passed down. Poison in the duke's plate."

Gerald thought furiously. If they did it, then he would lose all chance of any money, and, what was more important, possibly his life. He, Gerald, had arsenic left over after his abortive attempt this afternoon, an attempt he had no intention of telling them about.

"I'll do it," he said abruptly. "Plate passes in front of me, I calculate which is the duke's plate, nod to you, you create a diversion, I pop in the poison, and that's that. What about the death certificate?"

"Our doctor will do what he is told." Percy studied Gerald for a few moments and then said, "Very well. But make sure you do not fail. We'd better get Lady Macdonald along as well. The unhappier we keep our little duchess, the better, just in case. You go to Lady Macdonald and get her along."

"She may have other arrangements."

"When there's a chance of her keeping her claws in Ferrant?" sneered Percy. "She'll come."

"Who else?" asked Gerald. "I mean, who else is coming?"

"Old Mrs. Tregader and her granddaughter, Miss

Isabella, Mr. Fawley and his father, the duke and duchess, Lady Macdonald and yourself, and Mr. and Mrs. Tumley."

"Sounds awful," said Gerald, with feeling. "Now try to leave my quarters without being seen by anyone and I will call on Lady Macdonald."

It was, thought Alice, as they all gathered in Lord Werford's gloomy drawing room before supper, a party surely arranged in hell. First there was Lady Macdonald, seductive and blooming and witty, then there was Gerald, who kept smiling at her in a way her husband obviously did not like, while the gossipy Tumleys avidly watched everything. Then there was the walking tragedy of Isabella Tregader. Her parents had died and she was being brought out by her horror of a grandmother. Isabella was quite beautiful, but in a washed-out way, as if someone had taken a sponge over a fine painting. Everyone in society knew her grandmother had high ambitions for her. Isabella had been in love with an army captain who had been sent packing by old Mrs. Tregader. Mr. Fawley, thin, effeminate, waspish, and rich, had been chosen for her. Mrs. Tregader was very wealthy but a miser—and wanted more money for her coffers through her granddaughter. Mr. Fawley sat next to Isabella, and she listened to his compliments with her face averted.

Lord Werford approached Gerald and drew him aside. "In the pudding," he hissed.

"Why not the soup?" muttered Gerald.

"Because I want to enjoy my supper first," said Lord Werford, with mad logic.

"And how is our little duchess?" Lady Macdonald was asking Alice.

"Very well, I thank you," said Alice. "And how is our large Lady Macdonald?"

Lady Macdonald laughed merrily. "Ah, my child, I know that jealousy prompted that remark."

"Really?" said Alice, moving away. "And what prompted yours?"

"If I had known that woman was going to be here," said Gerald suddenly, next to Alice, "I would have warned you." He reflected grimly on the amount of persuasion he had to bring to bear on Lady Macdonald to get her to come, Lady Macdonald complaining that the way Ferrant had fled to his wife's side at the picnic had been humiliating.

"I would really rather not discuss her," said Alice. "Such a mystery about that pâté this afternoon."

"What mystery? Some dog near death found the stuff too rich and was put out of its misery."

"But such a pity you threw the jar on the fire," said Alice. "There could have been poison in it . . . and we could have taken it to the pharmacy and had it examined."

Gerald repressed a shudder. "We are not at war with the French anymore," he said lightly. "No reason to think they are trying to poison us."

"Still, it was strange. Edward said you were at a curricle race in Hammersmith."

"Edward Vere? Yes, I had the pleasure of meeting him there."

"Edward said you rode off before the start of the race. You were carrying a gun bag."

"Yes, I had to take my gun for repair."

"Most gentlemen send their servants on such an errand."

Gerald forced a laugh. "Gentlemen rub down their horses themselves, and see to their guns themselves, and trust either chore to a servant. Ah, I see we are about to go in for supper," he added, with relief.

The duke, being the highest in rank, led Alice in. To their surprise they found that Lord Werford favored the old-fashioned seating arrangements, that is, the ladies at one side of the long table and the gentlemen on the other.

"Quite American," said Alice to Isabella, who was placed next to her.

"Yes," agreed Isabella, "and in some places the ladies in America even dine separately from the men, drink a great deal, tell coarse stories, and laugh a lot." She surveyed the tablecloth in silence and then added, "I would *very* much like to be in America."

"Is there no chance of your going there?" asked Alice.

"There is no chance of anything in my life—except marriage to the man chosen for me by my grandmother," said Isabella. "I have a friend in Virginia, now Mrs. Harry Bellman. She was at the ladies' seminary in Bath with me. She writes to me often asking me to come. If Grandmama died, I would go, and I would sit and drink and laugh with the American ladies and be free. But Grandmama will not die. She will sit managing my life, horrible old toad."

All this was delivered in a rapid undertone. Alice looked nervously at Isabella. She thought that young lady looked on the point of a complete break-down.

"My engagement to Fawley is to be announced next week," went on Isabella. "I have prayed and prayed for God to strike Grandmama dead."

"And what are you ladies gossiping about?" came the arch voice of Mrs. Tumley on the other side of Alice.

"*We* do not gossip," said Alice coldly. "Only empty-headed women do *that*," and Mrs. Tumley turned away in a huff to speak to Lady Macdonald.

Lord Werford, at the head of the table, was so slow at serving out the various dishes that all his guests—with the exception of Percy and Gerald—wished he would adopt more modern methods and have his servants pass round the plates, because by the time he had carved and the plates were passed down the table, the food was nearly cold.

Alice looked across the table at her husband, who suddenly smiled sympathetically at her, as if to say, Yes, I know. All this is quite dreadful, and she smiled back at him.

Then she realized that Isabella was still talking. It was as if Isabella had never spoken of her troubles before, and, once started, could not stop. "I was in love with Captain Maltravers," she said. "But Grandmama put a stop to that. Captain Maltravers married Betty Dance, quite an undistinguished female of no looks and little dowry. He managed to meet me at a party and to whisper, 'Good-bye.'

" 'Wait,' I said, 'only wait. Grandmama cannot live forever.' But he said, and so bitterly that it nigh broke my heart, 'Old boot face will live for-ever.' So that is how I now think of her. Old boot face. Look at her!"

Mrs. Tregader was at the end of the table, eating her food with great sucking and chomping noises. Bits of food were clinging to her gown and to the collar of dirty diamonds around her neck.

Alice was distracted from Isabella's complaints as the voice of Lady Macdonald, extolling the joys of Paris, reached her ears. "Of course, the only place to dine is the Rocher de Cancalle in the Rue Mandar," she was saying. "The cook, Borel, formerly used to cook for Napoléon and he showed me his visitors' book. Such names! The Duke of Bedford, Charles James Fox, and Robespierre. Of course, some say Beauvilliers in the Rue de Richelieu is the finer, but I disagree."

"What amazes me," boomed Mrs. Tregader, "is that no sooner is the war over than the English flock over there and suddenly everything has got to be French."

"We weren't at war with their cooking or culture, Grandmama," said Isabella.

"Hark at miss!" jeered the old woman. "Don't you get saucy with me! I tell you, Fawley, a touch of the birch is what she needs to keep her in line."

This remark had the effect of causing a heavy, gloomy silence—broken finally by Lord Werford, who announced, "Floating island pudding," in the stentorian manner of an ostler outside a coaching inn announcing the destinations of the coaches.

Gerald felt a light sweat breaking out on his forehead. This was it. Now count. Plates passed down. First for Mr. Fawley, senior, next for his son, and now the next would be for the duke. It was a large helping.

"Oh, my stars and garters!" shouted Lord Werford suddenly, hopping up and down. While all stared at him, Gerald poured the arsenic powder into the duke's plate of pudding.

"Sorry," said Lord Werford. "Twinge of gout. Keep on passing the plates, Warby."

Gerald smiled and gave the poison-loaded plate of pudding to the duke.

The serving continued, everyone politely waiting until everyone else had been served. The duke picked up his spoon.

"I've got only a little bit," complained Mrs. Tregader. "You served the gentlemen first, Werford. I am very fond of floating island pudding."

The duke signaled to a footman who was standing ready to take away empty plates to the kitchen. "Take my plate to Mrs. Tregader with my compliments."

"No!" said Gerald. Alice looked at him. "I mean," he said, forcing a smile, "I am not hungry. Have mine, Mrs. Tregader."

"I'll have Ferrant's," said the old woman, who had already noticed the duke had the largest portion.

The footman took the duke's plate to Mrs. Tregader, lifted her plate, and brought it round to the duke.

"I say," said Percy suddenly, "this pudding's sour. Do not eat it."

Mrs. Tregader shoveled the confection into her mouth. "Bit spicy," she remarked between mouthfuls, "but tasty. Very tasty."

"I hope it chokes her," muttered Isabella.

Nobody else ate theirs. After the plates had been cleared away, the cover was removed and fruit and nuts and decanters placed on the polished surface of the table. Alice realized that as Lord Werford had no hostess and as she was the most senior in rank, it was her duty to rise and lead the ladies to the drawing room.

Mrs. Tregader had often complained of having a weak heart while being privately convinced she was as strong as an ox. But the weak heart was a reality, and the first convulsion that racked her body put an end to her and realized her granddaughter's prayers. Mrs. Tregader rolled under the table and then lay there, as dead as a doornail.

They all gathered around while the duke knelt to feel the old lady's pulse. "She's not really dead," said Isabella. "She's just playing dead. We had a dog who could do that." She looked wildly around and then collapsed into hysterics.

Lady Macdonald slapped her smartly on the face, and Isabella flung herself into Alice's arms and sobbed.

Alice soothed her, but all the while her eyes ranged round the guests. Fawley senior and Fawley junior were white and shaken. Lady Macdonald looked bored. Mrs. Tumley was gazing avidly from face to face, but then she always looked like that, constantly seeking out scandal. Gerald was a muddy color but quite composed. Werford and Percy were slumped in their chairs, both of them staring straight ahead.

"We had best take Miss Tregader home with us," said Alice when her husband rose to her feet. "She cannot be alone this night."

"Take the carriage and take her home now," said the duke. "I will stay here until the doctor arrives. And you stay as well, Warby," he snapped as Gerald moved toward the door. For one awful moment, Gerald thought the duke knew he had been guilty of poisoning the pudding, but then he quickly realized that the jealous duke did not want him to leave at the same time as Alice, in case he accompanied her home.

The rest of that evening Alice had her hands full with the weeping Isabella, who was now thinking God would strike *her* dead for her evil thoughts about her grandmother. Alice soothed her, saying sensibly over and over again that no one could wish anyone else dead. Isabella could now go to Virginia as soon as the funeral was over. She must bear up and think of that. It was all very sad, but Mrs. Tregader had been so very old. It was not as if she had died young, and, furthermore, Isabella need not wed the horrible Mr. Fawley after all. She talked on and on until Isabella's maid arrived with her luggage and Isabella finally went to bed, pale but composed; Alice sank down in a chair in her private sitting room, feeling wrung out and exhausted.

It was too much of a coincidence, she kept thinking. First the pâté, now the pudding. That pudding had been meant for the duke. Her scared thoughts ran round and round in her head.

The door opened and her husband stood on the threshold. Alice looked at him wide-eyed, as if seeing him for the first time. Fear for him made her rush across the room and throw her arms about him.

"Now this is what I call a welcome," said the duke, holding her close.

Alice leaned back in his arms and looked up into his face. "John, that pudding was meant for you. Then there was the pâté . . ."

"I do seem to lead a charmed life, do I not?" he

teased. "But how wonderful you should feel such concern for me."

"I have been a bad wife, John. . . . "

"Shhh." He put a hand over her lips. "The dog was a poor sick thing anyway, and Werford's doctor confirmed that Mrs. Tregader died of a heart attack. Furthermore, her own doctor was called by Fawley, who looked as if he had just lost the crown jewels, and he said that Mrs. Tregader had often complained of pains at her heart. He had suggested she try to eat less, but she would not heed his advice."

"But the shooting in the Park," said Alice when he took his hand away.

"Ah, that. Most odd. But I have no enemies. Hush, my dear, it has been a dreadful day. How is Miss Tregader?"

"Quieter now. She was consumed by guilt, but the realization that she does not need to marry Fawley after all has done wonders for her spirits."

His eyes hardened. "Damn all conniving parents and relatives who would force daughters into unhappy marriages."

"Ah, do not be so bitter," cried Alice. "In truth, I am *glad*, yes, glad, I did not marry Gerald, for I fear I do not even like him at all."

He crushed her to him and kissed her breathless.

She kissed him back with all her heart and soul, and he forgot she was a virgin, only knew that she was the most desirable woman he had ever held in his arms, and proceeded to make love to her with a mixture of expertise and blinding passion. He kissed her neck and the tops of her breasts until she moaned against him, so that with a triumphant laugh, he scooped her up in his arms and carried her through to her bedroom, falling onto the bed with her and removing her clothes as he kissed her and kissed her.

He left her for a moment to tear off his own clothes, before seizing her again and covering her nakedness with his own. Their bodies heaved and turned and clung until dawn came through the window and bleached the flames of the guttering candles. Alice eventually fell into an exhausted sleep wrapped closely in his arms.

He lay awake for a moment, looking up at the bed canopy. That she had been a virgin until this night was in no doubt. But her passion had matched his, at times had seemed to exceed his. He was grateful but puzzled. All gentlemen knew that ladies were incapable of passion. Only wantons and trollops were. He felt he had moved into strange territory, but he settled her head more comfortably on his chest before he, too, fell asleep.

During the next few days, the duke found himself wishing Isabella Tregader in hell. He had to admit to himself in his saner moments that his love for his wife had become an obsession. He wanted her every minute of the day, but every minute of the day appeared to be taken up with soothing Isabella, helping Isabella with the funeral arrangements, and driving Isabella to the lawyers, where that young lady was amazed to find out the extent of her fortune. He had not been able to share Alice's bed since that first hectic time, for Isabella had nightmares and called for Alice to sit by her bed. At last the duke found out from Isabella the name of her old nurse, who was now resident in Bath, drove there, brought the old lady back, and, with great relief, installed both nurse and Isabella in the late Mrs. Tregader's home.

Now he had his bride all to himself . . . and yet he found himself in the grip of the most burning jealousy. She *had* been in love with that cur, Warby, had she not? Had she given *him* such burning kisses? And so he finally made love to her in such a punishing way that she cried out he was hurting her, and he opened his mouth and said sourly, "I am sorry I cannot compete with your *first* lover," and Alice had become tearful and furious and the night had ended in disaster, with him stalking off to his own bedroom.

And he did not know it was this very insane jealousy of Gerald that kept Alice from confiding her fears in him. The more she thought about all those incidents, the more she became convinced that Gerald was trying to kill her husband. It was no use talking about it to John, she thought wearily, for he would only hear the very word, Gerald, and then begin to rant and rage and would not listen to anything else.

The day her husband went riding in the Row with Edward and he was thrown from his horse—and a jagged piece of metal was found by the groom wedged under the horse's saddle—Alice made up her mind. She would meet Gerald and tell him that if other incidents occurred, she would go to the authorities with her suspicions.

She knew the duke was to make a speech at the House of Lords that afternoon on the Irish question. Where to meet Gerald? She finally decided that St. James's Park was the best venue. The Park was no longer fashionable with the Quality. She wrote him a letter, sanded it, and sealed it.

"And let us hope that is the end of Gerald," she said to Oracle as the bird hopped about the floor. "To think I once loved Gerald!" The bird put its head on one side and regarded her with bright eyes. Alice laughed and handed him a grape. "Oracle, I sometimes think you are the only one who loves me."

Gerald read the letter with surprise and delight. Lord Werford's spies had reported that the duke and duchess were very much reconciled, but surely this letter showed things were different.

He was early for his appointment with Alice at the south end of the Park. Through the lime trees, he could see the red brick front of Buckingham House.

She had arranged to meet him at two o'clock. The bells of London began to chime the two strokes. On Horseguards, a lazy group of soldiers strolled past, magnificent in red and gold.

He did not see Alice arrive, for he had been searching for one of the duke's carriages. But she came on horseback, and he swung round in time to see her sliding deftly down from the saddle.

Alice tethered her horse to one of the hitching posts at the edge of Horseguards. She was looking very elegant in a blue velvet riding dress with a little jaunty hat on the side of her head.

"Alice!" cried Gerald, seizing her hands. She experienced a qualm of doubt, for the Gerald who was looking at her was in that moment the Gerald she had once known, happy and carefree. She disengaged her hands. "Those soldiers are staring at us," she said quietly. "Walk for a little with me under the trees."

"So to what do I owe the honor of this meeting?" asked Gerald.

Alice took a deep breath. "Gerald, I think . . . I know . . . that you are trying to kill my husband."

He put his hand on his heart, that stagy gesture she so much distrusted, and his eyes were limpid. "I? My heart, you must be mad!"

"I saw you," said Alice wearily. "I am sure it was you, in the Park, on the day of the shooting. You were wearing a wide-brimmed hat and a cloak, and I only saw your back, but I know it was you. You were walking away from those bushes, where the gun was found, with a canvas gun bag slung over your shoulder. Then there was the pâté. Why throw it in the fire? And then the supper party at Lord Werford's. Then I heard Ferrant had been tossed from his horse in the Row and a sharp piece of metal had been found under the saddle. Too many coincidences."

"I' faith, nothing to do with me," exclaimed Gerald angrily, angry that he had been found out. "Alice, you *know* me. We were to be married."

"But you have changed," said Alice sadly. "There is an air of coarseness, of untrustworthiness about you. It is no use arguing, Gerald. My husband is at the House this afternoon, and when he returns, I am going to insist he listen to my suspicions."

Gerald turned pale. News of the duke's duel had filtered to his ears. Already his mind was racing around, seeking a way out of his predicament. He had money enough from the advance from Werford. He could leave the country and lie low until everything had blown over. But still he protested his innocence—while Alice looked at him with a new hard cynicism in her eyes—and he found himself wondering how he could ever have been in love with her.

At last, he said, "Alice, for the love I bear you, I will leave London and go abroad again. But you will find out you were wrong. I bear no malice toward your husband. I envy him."

The hard look left Alice's eyes. "Oh, Gerald, please do go away."

Alice had left the duke's town house at one o'clock, first to call on Mrs. Duggan, which is where she had told the servants she was going.

This the duke learned after he had looked in at the newly decorated drawing room in search of her. She was not there, but Oracle was, preening himself in his large cage and regarding the duke with bright, intelligent eyes.

The duke looked at the bird with amusement. "Where is your mistress?" he asked.

"Gerald," said the bird. "Love . . . Gerald. Love, love, love. Only one that loves me."

The bird then cocked its head on one side and looked at the duke hopefully, expecting a grape in reward.

The duke stood and stared at the bird, and then he reached out a hand and jerked the bell rope.

Hoskins, the butler, came in. "Where is the duchess?" demanded the duke harshly.

"Her Grace went riding. Her Grace said she would call on Mrs. Duggan."

"Why not in a carriage? Where is her maid?"

"In the servants' hall."

The duke studied his butler with icy eyes. "Did

my wife receive a letter from anyone this day? Or did someone's footman call?"

Hoskins had been dreading this. He stared straight ahead and said woodenly, "Sir Gerald Warby's man called with a letter, Your Grace."

The duke walked straight past him and up to his wife's rooms—and straight to her writing desk. There was a crumpled sheet of paper on the top of it with a broken seal. He smoothed it out and read,

> My dear, It is my pleasure to wait on you in St. James's Park, as you requested, at two this afternoon at the south end near Horseguards. As you know, your slightest wish is my command, Your Loving Servant, Gerald.

The duke ran downstairs, calling for his racing curricle to be brought round.

Gerald, standing with Alice by her horse, saw the duke speeding toward them out of the corner of his eye. "Give me something of yours, Alice," he begged. "Your handkerchief. Something to take with me on my exile."

She drew out her handkerchief and handed it to him. He pressed it to his lips. And having noticed that the duke had just witnessed this affecting scene, he suddenly took to his heels and ran off as hard as he could. He hoped Alice had a rotten time trying to explain her gesture. Serve her right! Now home to pack as quickly as possible, before Ferrant came looking for him.

The duke marched up to Alice. "Oh, John," said Alice, with a smile. "It must look very odd, but I can explain."

"Get in the carriage," he snapped. He tied her horse onto the back of the curricle. Alice got in. He jumped in beside her and picked up the reins.

"Please listen," begged Alice.

"Not a word until we are in private," said the duke. He was white with rage and his lips were set in a thin line.

He drove home at great speed, then shouted to his servant to put the carriage away, and, taking Alice's arm in a firm grip, he marched her into the library.

"John, should you not be in the House?" said Alice weakly. "Your speech . . ."

"My speech be damned!" He drew Gerald's letter out of his pocket. "You sent for your lover," he hissed, "thinking I would never find out about it."

"I can explain," said Alice wretchedly. "Gerald is trying to kill you!"

"What?"

"He is trying to kill you. The shot in the Park . . . The man I saw walking away from the scene looked so like Gerald . . . The pâté, Mrs. Tregader . . ."

"Oh, for heaven's sake. Do you take me for a fool? What Gothic nonsense is this? While your bird cries, 'Gerald,' and 'love, love, love,' do you expect me to believe such rubbish? I would dearly like to call Warby out, but there has been enough scandal. You will remove to Clarendon and you will stay there, guarded by my servants, until I decide what to do with you."

"John, for pity's sake, hear me."

"No, you wanton, I have listened to you enough." He rang the bell and told the footmen to send in Mr. Shadwell, the secretary.

Mr. Shadwell came in, his eyes flickering to and then away from Alice, who was now weeping.

"Mr. Shadwell," said the duke heavily, "I trust your discretion. Her Grace is to be conducted to Clarendon as soon as possible. She is to be guarded on the journey. At Clarendon she is to keep to the house and gardens. She is not to go beyond the gardens, nor is she to receive any visitors, particularly her parents. Do I make myself clear?"

"Yes, Your Grace," said Mr. Shadwell, thinking gloomily that he had become the duke's secretary to further his own political ambitions, not to act as jailer to the duchess.

"Very well. Instruct the maids to pack Her Grace's belongings and put that hell bird in its carrying cage and get it out of my sight." He swung round and faced Alice. "You will stay here until Mr. Shadwell tells you the carriage is ready. You will ride inside on the journey, Mr. Shadwell, and see that no one approaches or speaks to Her Grace. Come, Mr. Shadwell. We have much to do."

He marched out of the library and waited until his secretary had also left the room before locking the library door.

Alice sat huddled on a sofa in the middle of the room. Books in serried ranks stared down at her, all the wisdom of the ages, and none of it able to help her in her predicament.

By the time a highly embarrassed and miserable Mr. Shadwell unlocked the door to tell Alice that the traveling coach was waiting outside, she was red-eyed but composed. The beginning of anger against the duke was lending her courage.

The duke was nowhere in sight as Alice walked out to the carriage with Mr. Shadwell on one side, the maid, Betty, on the other, and a footman carrying the squawking Oracle in his cage behind.

Mr. Shadwell came across the first test of his new duties in the shape of Mrs. Duggan, who was standing, open-mouthed, with her maid, watching the procession.

"Faith, are you leaving us?" she cried.

"Her Grace is unwell," said Mr. Shadwell firmly, "and is not able to speak to anyone."

Alice's step faltered, but the secretary took her arm in a firm grip and urged her toward the carriage. "Like a prisoner," as Mrs. Duggan told her cronies, Dunfear and Donnelly, later.

Gerald had just finished packing. His manservant was guarding the downstairs door with a blunderbuss. Gerald heard voices below and stiffened in fright. Then he heard footsteps ascending the stairs, cursed his manservant under his breath, and slammed his bedroom door shut on the evidences of his packing. He was standing in the middle of his sitting room, feverishly priming a pistol, when Lord Werford and Percy walked into the room.

"That's our man," said Lord Werford, highly pleased. "You are doing fine work, Warby."

This was the last thing Gerald had expected and he smiled weakly at the unlovely pair.

Lord Werford rubbed his pudgy hands. "So because of your little rendezvous with the duchess, the jealous duke has banished her to the country and stays alone in London. Well done, Warby."

It was on the tip of Gerald's tongue to burst out with the news that Alice had accused him of trying to murder Ferrant, but he bit back the words as his mind worked busily. Alice could not have told the duke of her suspicions. Either that or the jealous duke would not listen. If he, Gerald, told them of Alice's suspicions, they would either order him to get rid of her as well, or they might decide to get rid of him and do the deed themselves.

"I arranged the meeting with the duchess," said Gerald, lying quickly, "and then made sure the duke knew about it."

"Very clever, Warby," drawled Percy. "A man after our own heart. But we have decided to help you. The trouble is that you have been rushing, hurly-burly, into things. Planning is what is needed."

"Planning?" echoed Gerald stupidly, for he still could not believe he was to get off so easily.

"Yes, planning," said Lord Werford. "Old Lord Rother at Streatham was an old friend of the late duke's. After being a bachelor and something of a recluse, he has recently married a flighty widow and the widow wants to entertain. To that end, she is giving a breakfast in the gardens of Blackberry Hill House at Streatham in two weeks' time. Now Blackberry Hill House, as you may have heard, is a miserable Gothic folly that the miserly Lord Rother did nothing to maintain before his marriage. Repairs are to begin on the ugly place next month. In the meanwhile, bits of masonry keep tumbling off the building. Percy here has been cultivating the company of the new Lady Rother. The breakfast, which begins at three in the afternoon, will be, as I said, laid out in the gardens, and Percy has persuaded her that the table with the most important guests should be next to the building under the west front—and the west front carries some nasty and crumbling gargoyles.

"Your job is to gain entry to the house with a bag of mason's tools. Percy here will see that the seating arrangements are correct. You will chisel loose one of those gargoyles, the one directly above the duke's head, and send it crashing down."

"But how do I get into the house?" asked Gerald. "Would it not be easier if you simply engineered an invitation for me?"

"No, I will tell the staff that a mason is to call to inspect the building. You, in appropriate dress, will call at the door of the servants' quarters and will be admitted without any trouble."

"Sounds almost too easy," said Gerald doubtfully.

"It will be easy."

"But what about Ferrant? He won't feel like going to parties and things after the breakup of his marriage."

Lord Werford rubbed his hands again. "I think his great pride will force him to try to appear as normal as possible. Now we will leave you. We are most pleased with you."

The Duke of Ferrant, turning the corner of South Molton Street on his road to Gerald's apartment, saw the stout figure of Lord Werford and the prim figure of Percy walking away from the building. What had that pair been doing calling on Gerald Warby?

But he marched up to the door and hammered on it. Gerald's manservant, now unarmed, for Gerald had told him the panic was over, looked at the duke in dismay.

"Your master?" demanded the duke.

"Not at home," said the manservant quickly.

The duke thrust him aside and climbed the stairs. Gerald was sprawled in an armchair, celebrating with a glass of brandy, which fell from his suddenly nerveless fingers as the duke loomed in the open doorway.

"I am come," said the duke evenly, "to tell you that if you ever dare to approach or speak to my wife again, I will shoot you dead."

"What w-was I to d-do?" stammered Gerald. "She wrote to me, begging me to meet her."

"Where is the handkerchief she gave you?"

Gerald thrust his hand in his pocket and held it out. The duke snatched it.

"I would like to beat your face to a pulp, Warby," he said, "but there has been scandal enough. Heed my words or I will kill you." The duke turned to go. "Did I see Werford and that son of his leaving here?"

"Not here," said Gerald. "Fitzwilliam lives next door and he knows Werford."

And thank God that's over, thought Gerald, as the door closed behind the duke, and thank God I'm still alive. But somewhere in his mind, he wished that Werford and Percy had not called, that he had left, but as soon as he had heard them out, he thought again of all the money they would give him. He was sure they would give him the money and then try to kill him and take it back, but he meant to leave the country for once and for all before that happened.

He poured himself another glass of brandy and drank it down in one gulp. And then he thought of Lady Macdonald. He would call on her and let her think he had deliberately engineered Alice's disgrace. She might even give him more money! His conscience gave another twinge, but he put it down to indigestion.

Chapter Eight

HUMPHREY DOGGET-BLYTHE, "Doggie" to his friends, looked like a whipped cur. In the cruel world of society, it was not only young ladies who were press-ganged into unsuitable marriages but young men as well.

Humphrey was the victim of domineering and ambitious parents who had teamed up with another set of equally domineering parents with a marriageable daughter. So in spite of Humphrey's bewildered protests that the Honorable Mary Sutworth was a long-nosed, Friday-faced antidote, he soon found himself wed to her. At university and then in the army, he had experienced freedom. He had been popular and had led an easygoing life. Now he was nagged by Mary from morning until night. Her voice had a particularly shrill edge that reminded him of an unoiled garden gate.

Edward Vere, calling on his old friend, was appalled to see the once cheerful and plump Doggie of the army reduced to a thin, careworn man who jumped at his own shadow. Edward could only count his blessings in having found his Lucy. Ferrant was miserable, and now Doggie was miserable. While Lucy talked to Mary, Edward suggested that Humphrey show him the garden.

142

"My only consolation." Humphrey sighed as they strolled across the lawns. "I wish I could reenlist."

"Why don't you?" asked Edward.

"Can't," said Humphrey miserably. He jerked his head in the direction of the house.

Edward wanted to say that it was time Humphrey asserted himself, but he had only the day before received a stinging lecture from Ferrant on the impertinent folly of friends poking their unwanted noses into other friends' marriages.

"Going to this breakfast of Rother's tomorrow?" asked Edward instead.

"Yes," said Humphrey. "Mary says we are going."

"Humphrey! Come here!" called an imperative voice from the house.

Humphrey trailed back. "I did not give you leave to go wandering off like that," said Mary, meeting him at the French windows.

"Sorry, dear," mumbled Humphrey.

"Doggie was showing me the roses," said Edward.

"I will not have anyone calling him by that ridiculous nickname," said Mary.

She was a tall, thin, flat-chested woman, and the nose Humphrey so disliked had a habit of developing a pink spot on the end of it when she was displeased, rather in the manner of a sort of marital beacon warning of reefs ahead.

"We really must go," said Lucy brightly.

"No, don't go," pleaded Humphrey. "Haven't seen Edward this age. Haven't seen anyone this age."

"Don't be ridiculous, Humphrey. You are always being ridiculous," said Mary. "Simpkins! Call Mr. Vere's carriage. We shall be pleased to entertain you again, Mr. Vere, but in future, write to apprise us of your visit. We do not like impromptu visits."

"Oh, poor Doggie." Edward sighed as he and Lucy made their way home. "Another unhappy man."

Humphrey listened for the rest of that day to strictures from Mary on his "vulgar" friends. Edward was so coarse, more like a Billingsgate porter than a gentleman. And Lucy was vulgar and made no effort to conceal her pregnancy, as any lady ought to do.

It was while she was talking that a little glow of comfort began to spread through Humphrey's soul. He would kill himself, that very evening. He would probably go to hell, but he might find some jolly fellows there to play cards with. Mary prided herself on being good and she would probably go to heaven, but he did not relish the idea of a heaven full of Marys. For once, he felt an inner strength, and the flow of her voice broke on the rock of his decision and swept out past his shoulders to the garden. Hanging would be fine and tidy and quiet, thought Edward. There was a hook on a beam in the tack room that would do perfectly. Provided he was cool and calm about it all and made sure the knot was under his ear so that his neck would break immediately, it should not be too bad.

Mary liked to retire to bed at nine in the evening, after a shared supper of dry toast and tea. All he had to do was to say, in his usual way, that he would follow her upstairs.

No sooner had she planted a cold kiss on his brow, no sooner had the light from her bed candle wavered past the first landing, than he was off and running to the stables.

He slid into the warm mustiness of the tack room,

lit an oil lamp, and set it on the floor. He found a coil of rope and fashioned it into a noose. He stood on a chair and fastened the rope competently to the hook and then tested the noose. Perfect.

Now for welcome death. But first, he really ought to say his prayers and ask God for mercy on his soul.

He knelt down in the middle of the tack room—beside the chair and under the shadow of the noose—clasped his hands, bent his head, and closed his eyes.

"Have you lost something, you great ninny?" came Mary's voice from the doorway. Surely to even the most insensitive woman the sight of her husband kneeling in prayer, under a gently swinging noose, would have told its own story. But Mary had been blessed with a hide tougher than that of the usual human being and only saw a bumbling and ineffectual husband who had dropped something.

Superstitiously Humphrey felt that this was God's way of punishing him for having tried to commit suicide. As he got to his feet, he said in a squeaky voice that he had dropped his ruby pin earlier and thought he might have left it in the tack room.

"How could you drop something in the tack room when you have not been in it all day?" demanded Mary. "It's a good thing I saw you go over here from the upstairs window or you might have been looking all night. And tell the stable boys to take that noose down. Playing hangman can lead to disaster. Come along, sir. You have been looking peaky all day and a good dose of paraffin is what you need to bring you to rights. Come along."

"Yes, dear," said Humphrey.

* * *

The Duke of Ferrant was not looking forward to the breakfast at Lord Rother's, but then he did not look forward to anything these days. He had made an appointment with his lawyers to discuss a divorce from Alice, but then he had canceled it at the last minute, for he thought that if Alice were free, she might immediately marry Gerald Warby, and he could not bear that.

It was a fine sunny day when he drove to Streatham. When he arrived, the first person he saw after he had been welcomed by the Rothers was Lady Macdonald. He bowed to her but did not go to join her. He would not add to the gossip that surrounded him.

He almost did not recognize his old friend, Humphrey Dogget-Blythe, in the careworn man who was plodding along behind his wife, carrying her fan and shawl. But Doggie saw him and his face lit up in a sweet smile.

"Is it really you, Doggie?" asked the duke.

Mary looked him up and down with cold eyes. "Kindly address my husband by his proper name," she snapped.

"My love," quavered Humphrey, "this is His Grace, the Duke of Ferrant. Allow me to introduce you."

Mary simpered and curtsied. A duke was a duke. "You must forgive me, Your Grace," she gushed. "I thought for a moment you were one of my husband's rough army friends."

"I knew your husband in the army," said the duke, looking at her with dislike. He turned to Humphrey. "Well, how goes the world? You are but a shadow of your former self."

"He ate much too much," said Mary before Humphrey could open his mouth. "I put him on a diet of vinegar and potatoes."

The duke bowed and moved away, vowing to try to have a word with Humphrey in private later.

He then met Lord Werford and Percy, but as he disliked them both, he only exchanged a few words before joining more congenial company.

They were then told to take their places. High above the babble sounded Mary's voice. "I cannot sit in the sun. This place card says I should sit *here*, but it is in full sunlight and my skin is amazingly delicate."

At the same time, the duke had just discovered that he was to be seated at the top table, in the shadow of the house, next to Lady Macdonald. He approached Mary. "You may take my place, ma'am," he said, "and I will sit with your husband."

Mary looked gratified. Everyone would see her at the top table. To Humphrey's relief, she thanked the duke and swept off.

"Oh, God," said Lord Werford to Percy. "It's all gone wrong. You'll need to get up to the roof and tell that fool Warby to leave the gargoyle alone."

Percy moved to the doorway of the house. He found his way blocked by Lady Rother, a sprightly widow with a hard, ambitious eye. "Where are you going?" she asked.

Percy murmured something about needing to visit the "necessary house."

"A footman will conduct you there and bring

you back," said Lady Rother testily. "I would like everyone to be seated."

She summoned a footman and gave him instructions, and so Percy was conducted to the privy while the footman waited outside, and then the footman escorted him back to the guests. Percy looked across at his uncle and spread his hands in a gesture of resignation.

"Horrible place, isn't it?" said Humphrey to the duke. Both men surveyed the Gothic building, where gargoyles sprouted out at all angles from the roof.

"Badly in need of repair," remarked the duke. "A friend of mine was here last month and said a piece of masonry nearly landed on his head when he was walking in the garden."

"Do you believe in God?" asked Humphrey.

The duke looked at him in surprise. Everyone in the beginning of the nineteenth century believed in God. "Yes, why do you ask?" he demanded.

"Sometimes when one is in great pain," said Humphrey, "one prays and prays for help . . . but nothing happens."

A look of pain crossed the duke's own face, but he said soothingly, "Oh, whatever happens to us is meant to happen."

Up on the roof in the sunshine, Gerald chiseled happily away at the gargoyle, happy because he could not see his target, although knowing it would undoubtedly land on the duke's head. Not seeing him made it seem more impersonal. There was nowhere else it could fall. It was a nasty gargoyle anyway, its head like a serpent, its huge, gaping mouth opened in a stone snarl.

Underneath, Mary's nose flashed its angry warning, but her husband did not seem to notice. He was talking to the duke. Humphrey should have told her he was friendly with a duke. How like him to be secretive! She would punish him for this!

"I should not discuss my wife," Humphrey was saying, "but I am at the end of my tether."

"Then get away from her," said the duke. "Join the army again."

"I cannot. Mary holds the purse strings."

"Look, old friend, I cannot bear to see you like this. I shall buy you a commission. In fact, do not go home after this. Come back with me. You would be free."

"Free," echoed Humphrey. And then his face fell and he shook his head sadly. "You don't know what Mary's like. She would follow me to the ends of the earth to get her revenge. I tell you what, Ferrant, I tried to kill myself last night, but she even stopped me doing that."

"Was she not appalled at the extremes she had driven you to?"

"Would you believe that when she found me saying my last prayers on the tack room floor, with a noose swinging above my head, she thought I had lost something?"

The duke looked across the guests to Mary and said, "Yes. But you must not do such a thing again. There is always hope."

"What hope? A bolt from heaven will strike her down?"

Lady Macdonald was seated next to Mary but was confining her attentions to the gentleman on her other side. The gentleman on Mary's other side had exchanged a few words with her and then turned away with relief, feeling he had done his duty for the meal. So Mary sat alone. No Humphrey to nag. Her temper was becoming worse by the minute.

Humphrey looked across the garden; his eyes met his wife's basilisk stare, and he trembled.

The duke said something, and he turned his head. Then there was a rending scream and he looked across again. Where Mary had been sitting was a large gargoyle.

He jumped to his feet and struggled through the milling, screaming, and swooning guests. It looked as if Mary had been *swallowed* up by the gargoyle. Its stone mouth had engulfed her, what was left of her crushed under that terrible maw.

Humphrey began to laugh hysterically and was still laughing when the duke reached him and led him away.

Alice wandered about the gardens of Clarendon followed by her maid, Betty. Her parents had tried to call several times but had been turned away by the efficient Mr. Shadwell. Alice turned her head and said impatiently, "There is no need to follow me everywhere, Betty. I wish to be alone."

"Don't go doing anything silly, Your Grace," said Betty gloomily. "I would lose my job."

"You will not lose your job," said Alice testily. "I have no doubt His Grace will divorce me and then you will be in my employ as usual."

Betty reluctantly withdrew. Alice walked idly over to the stables. She usually walked about the grounds for most of the day, hoping to exhaust herself so that by nightfall she would fall into a deep sleep and forget about the duke.

A small, wizened groom came staggering past,

carrying a bale of hay. Alice started in surprise. "Sam?" she said.

The groom stopped and put down the hay. "You are Sam, are you not?" asked Alice. "You worked for my parents."

"Yes, Your Grace."

"I remember, you took that letter to Sir Gerald for me."

"In a way, Your Grace."

"What do you mean, Sam?"

He scratched his head. "You probably know now, Your Grace. Your parents called back the footman when he was on the road to the stables and read that letter—and went to see Sir Gerald themselves."

"Ah, yes," said Alice bitterly. "And they told Sir Gerald that I was in love with His Grace."

"Not 'zactly," said Sam, reaching for the bale again.

"Stay. What do you mean?"

"Shouldn't be talking," muttered Sam.

"I command you."

"That footman, he went with Mr. and Mrs. Lacey. He heard them say they would pay Mr. Warby a large sum of money if he went away."

"Which," said Alice in a small voice, "he accepted."

"That he did."

"Thank you, Sam."

Alice moved away, her heart heavy. The final confirmation of Gerald's perfidy. Now she was trapped here in the country, and even now he might be trying to murder her husband.

She looked back at the house. Mr. Shadwell was standing on the terrace, watching her.

She turned away from the house and leaned her back against the branches of an oak tree.

"Don't look up," said an urgent Irish voice above her head. "It's me, Donnelly."

She opened her mouth, but he said, "Don't speak. He's watching from the terrace. Me and Dunfear and Mrs. Duggan are at the George and Dragon in the village. We tried to see you but were turned away. So here's the plan. If you can get out of the gardens and as far as the wall of the estate, there's a broken bit of wall about one hundred yards west of the south lodge. Be there at two this morning and we'll be there in a closed carriage to pick you up. Now back to the house with you before they become suspicious."

Alice pretended to go to sleep that night, but she lay awake, listening to the rumble of snores from Betty, who slept in a little dressing room on a truckle bed adjoining the bedroom.

At midnight, she rose and dressed quietly. She dared not take any luggage with her. She put a cloak on and raised the hood to cover her bright hair. She crept down the main staircase and then stopped on the first landing. A footman was sleeping in a chair in front of the door.

Alice moved very slowly, down and across the hall and into the Yellow Saloon, which she knew had French windows opening onto the terrace. To her relief, the windows were not locked but simply bolted on the inside. She eased the bolt back and opened the window, her heart in her mouth as it gave an ominous creak.

Outside lay a vista of moon-washed lawns—and freedom!

She took to her heels and ran.

By the time she reached the wall of the estate, she was feeling exhausted because the south wall was several miles from the house. She felt her way along the wall, stumbling through briars that tore at her cloak and stubbing her toes on fallen bits of stone from the estate wall.

At last she heard the gentle whinny of horses and could make out the black shape of a carriage through the broken section of wall.

With a glad cry, she scrambled over the stones and wrenched open the carriage door.

"And now," said Mrs. Duggan, "you'd better tell us what you've been doing."

At breakfast in a posting house on the road to London, Alice wearily told her rescuers over again about the attempts on the duke's life and how he had not believed her. "And I had to leave Oracle behind," mourned Alice, "for the bird would have squawked and alerted the servants when I was escaping. I hope they treat it well, but Betty has a fondness for the bird and I am sure she will see that no one harms it."

"If it hadn't been for that silly bird, your husband might have listened to you," said Mrs. Duggan. "But all we can do is this. We'll need to disguise ourselves and watch the duke's house, and try to foil any other attempts."

"How can we disguise ourselves and wait outside his house?" demanded Alice. "The servants would come out and ask us our business."

"We'll think of something," said Mrs. Duggan. "I always do, at any rate."

* * *

Ten days later the duke stood at the window of the drawing room of his town houses staring bleakly out into the street. He had been to Clarendon and back looking for his absent wife. He had called on Sir Gerald and had threatened him. If Alice even approached him, he was to report to him immediately. Lucy had been distressed but said she had not heard anything from Alice. Alice's parents were distraught, not helped by a lecture from the duke in which he had told them that they had destroyed their daughter's life.

Somewhere in England was Alice, without money, without luggage. Where could she have gone?

Hoskins entered the room. "Those strolling players are back again, Your Grace. Shall I send one of the servants to move them on?"

"No, leave them," said the duke curtly. Yes, they were there again, that odd troupe. An old, fat woman banged a tambourine, a thin man in a slouch hat played the flute while the Pierrot and Columbine danced, the Pierrot in his harlequin costume with his face hidden under a black mask, the masked Columbine in ballet skirt and spangled top who reminded him achingly of Alice, despite her straggling red hair.

In the street below, the Pierrot circled the Columbine and muttered, "Well, sure now, your husband's at the window so he's still alive."

"But for how long?" murmured Alice. "And he is bound to become suspicious of us sooner or later."

"Your own mother wouldn't recognize you in that red wig," said Mr. Donnelly, who was playing Pierrot.

The duke went out in the afternoon, and Lord Dunfear, in his slouch hat, hired a hack and followed the duke's carriage, then returned to Mrs. Duggan's to say the duke was in the House of Lords.

"That should keep him safe for a couple of hours," sighed Mrs. Duggan, massaging her feet. "Do you know, I'm thinking we've been wasting our time following the wrong person."

"What do you mean?" asked Alice.

"Why, we should have been following Warby to see what he gets up to. It's proof we need."

"I'll do that," said Mr. Donnelly, rising and stretching. "Good idea. You all wait here."

He was lucky enough to find Gerald just leaving his lodgings, and, pulling his hat down over his eyes, he followed him. Gerald set out in the direction of the city with Mr. Donnelly in pursuit. He went into a coffeehouse in Cheapside, and, after a moment's hesitation, Mr. Donnelly followed him in.

A brief glance was enough to tell him that Gerald had joined Lord Werford and his son, Percy, in a booth. Mr. Donnelly slid into the next booth and strained his ears, breaking off only to order a tankard of Dog's Nose.

"I can't do anything at the moment," he heard Gerald say petulantly. "I am sure he is having me watched in case that wife of his turns up on my doorstep."

"But you can," said Percy in his mincing voice. "We have managed to get a copy of the key to the back door of Ferrant's town house. The maid who is walking out with our servant will leave the door unbolted. She thinks she is letting in her lover. You arm yourself, go straight to his bedroom and shoot him, and then let yourself out. Simple."

"Something will go wrong," said Gerald, raising his voice and then lowering it so that Mr. Donnelly had to strain to hear his next words. "Have I not tried and tried? And what happens? Some dog eats the poisoned pâté at that picnic, Mrs. Tregader eats the poisoned pudding meant for the duke, and that gargoyle falls and kills someone else after I had spent hours up on Lord Rother's roof hacking away. So what is going to happen this time? I tell you something will go wrong."

"You'd better do it," said Percy silkily, "or it will be the worse for you."

Gerald groaned. "So what time?"

"Two in the morning," said Lord Werford. "He is not going anywhere tonight, so he has no reason to be in bed late. Here is the key. As soon as Percy here is duke, you'll get your money."

Mr. Donnelly goggled. He must tell the others. The duke must be warned.

But when he returned, despite her horror to learn that Lord Werford and his son were behind the attempts on the duke's life, Mrs. Duggan was adamant in her refusal to tell the duke. "What if he doesn't listen to us, the way he did not listen to his wife? No, we will catch Warby in the act."

The duke tossed and turned but could not sleep. Faintly, from down below, came the shrill sound of a pipe and the steady beat of a tambourine. Those odd strolling players and that Columbine who reminded him of Alice. How odd that they were still there. He had ordered his servants to pay them well. No doubt they felt they were giving him a free concert.

His thoughts turned again to Alice and her mad story of Warby trying to kill him. But the blinding jealousy he had felt that day was fading. All he knew was that he would do anything, promise anything, if only he could have Alice back. His mind turned back to her tale of attempted murder. Yes, there had been that odd shooting in the Park, then pâté, then that odd business with Mrs. Tregader, and then the gargoyle, which would have crushed him to death had he not changed places with Doggie's wife. But it was all coincidence, he thought fretfully. But if Alice came back, it did not matter what lies she told him, he would accept them all. Where was she? Was she lying cold and dead in a ditch somewhere?

He fell into an uneasy sleep at last.

"The door's locked," said Mr. Donnelly frantically. "He's locked it behind him."

"It's got glass panes. Stand back!" said Mrs. Duggan.

She swung her heavy tambourine at the glass pane near the lock and shattered it. Dunfear leaned in and turned the handle. "Fast, Alice," hissed Mrs. Duggan. "Donnelly's got the gun. Get us to the duke's bedchamber. Oh, hurry!"

Gerald ran silently about upstairs, opening door after door. He had been told where the duke's bedchamber was but had lost his way in the dark. At last he opened a door and saw a figure lying in a four-poster bed with the curtains drawn back. With shaking hands, he fumbled and lit a lantern he had brought with him and held it high, the weak rays shining across the room and on the sleeping duke's face.

With a sigh of relief, he set the lantern on the floor and raised the pistol. At that moment the duke opened his eyes and sat up.

It took a split second for the duke to see Gerald, to realize in that awful moment that Alice had told nothing but the truth. Gerald's hand wavered. It was one thing to shoot at a man from behind the shelter of bushes in the Park, another to gun him down at close range.

And the next second, Mr. Donnelly took careful aim from the doorway and shot Gerald dead while the duke stared in amazement at the troupe of strolling players, and then at the redheaded Columbine who was tearing off her mask and red wig, who was crying, "Oh, John, do you believe me now?"

Chapter Nine

LORD WERFORD AND PERCY had not gone to bed. They were waiting to hear from Sir Gerald that the duke was dead.

"And then what do we do with him?" asked Percy.

"Thought of something," said his father, and looked away.

Percy yawned and stretched. "At least suspicion won't fall on us. Everyone will think Warby was so madly in love with Alice that he shot him. I wonder if it ever crossed his mind that he would be the first person the law picked up."

"That one will probably have an alibi all ready," remarked his father.

Percy chuckled. "We're the alibi. It was all arranged. We're to say he was with us."

"The fool! As inheritors of the dukedom, the last thing we want to be is associated with Warby."

"So what are you going to do with him?"

Lord Werford rose and went to the sideboard, lifted a decanter of port, and held it up. "This is poisoned," he said. "One glass of this and he's out of our lives."

"And out of his own life, too," said Percy, and

sniggered. He cocked his head to one side. "Devil of a noise approaching. Not another riot."

"Lean out the window," said Lord Werford, "and tell me what you see."

Percy opened the window, bent forward, and looked down into the street. Torches and lanterns were bobbing and shining on the uniforms of the militia, all armed to the teeth.

"Well?" demanded Lord Werford's voice behind him.

But Percy did not reply. A feeling of apprehension was beginning to seize him. Down the street the soldiers marched—and then stopped outside the street door below.

Percy swung round, his face ashen. "They're here. They've come here. The soldiers. They've come for *us*!"

A banging on the door sounded from below and a great cry of, "Open in the king's name."

Lord Werford rose and went to the sideboard. He poured two glasses of port and held one out to his son.

Scandal rocked London the following day as the news spread and spread; Mrs. Duggan busily added fuel to the rumors by saying the duke was aware all along of the attempts on his life and had sent the duchess, guarded, to the country for her protection.

Lady Macdonald left for Paris. Although she had known nothing about the attempts on Ferrant's life, she had paid Warby a large sum of money and was afraid that the authorities would descend on her to ask the reason why if her bank ever revealed that information to them.

The duke was remorseful. He swore to Alice that

he would never, ever raise his voice to her again, would never disbelieve anything she said, and was such a tender and considerate husband that Alice was quickly able to recover from her own shock at the death of Gerald—and from her guilt at having ever known or loved such a man.

Betty, the maid, arrived back from Clarendon, bearing Oracle in his cage, explained that the bird had been in poor health after Alice had left, but that it had transpired that the groom, Sam, had turned out to have a way with birds and so Oracle had been put into his care.

Mrs. Duggan, Lucy, Edward, Lord Dunfear, and Mr. Donnelly were constant visitors, all reliving the adventures, and much as the duke would have liked more time alone with his wife, he was so grateful to Alice's Irish friends in particular that he always gave them a welcome.

"Poor Doggie is on his way to America," said Edward one day, "and does not know that his wife was murdered."

"Oh, dear," said Alice. "Isabella has gone to America as well and does not know the reason for her grandmother's death, either. We must write to them."

At that moment, Humphrey Dogget-Blythe was having his first dinner in the captain's cabin despite having been at sea for a week. He had fallen prey to dreadful seasickness and this day was the first that he had begun to feel human again, and, what was more, actually hungry.

It struck him as he sat down to table that he could eat what he liked. There was no Mary to criticize him. Mary would never allow him to drink anything stronger than tea or lemonade. The captain's claret, thought Humphrey, half closing his eyes as he savored it, was excellent.

Then he had time to take stock of his companions. Apart from the captain and the officers of the *Belle Rose*, there was a clergyman, small and precise, wearing his black clericals and an old-fashioned wig, a Virginian tobacco merchant who looked more scholar than merchant, and a pale and beautiful young lady called Isabella Tregader, who, he learned afterward, was traveling alone with her maid.

Over dinner, he appreciated her beauty in an intellectual sort of way, but that was all. Humphrey had never been at ease with the ladies, and, after his marriage, he privately thought that even under the most beautiful exterior probably lurked a hellcat.

It was only gentlemanly, however, to talk to Isabella, but she answered all questions in monosyllables and with lowered eyes.

The following day was relatively calm and sunny, and Humphrey felt like a new man. He was strolling on the deck when he saw Isabella coming toward him with her maid following behind.

Humphrey raised his hat and said it was a fine day. Isabella blushed and agreed.

Encouraged by her shyness and by the calm weather, Humphrey said that he was bound for Virginia. No, he did not know anyone there but had some letters of introduction.

At that moment, the captain came up and suggested they might like to sit on the deck. Both were suddenly struck with shyness, which the captain took for assent. Two large Jacobean armchairs upholstered in tapestry were carried out from the captain's sitting room and placed on the deck, and the couple sat down side by side. There was something so odd, so novel about sitting in such landlubber furniture on a sailing ship, watching the sun sparkling on the waves, that their shyness suddenly went. Isabella told Humphrey of the death of her grandmother, and Humphrey told her of the death of his wife—and both agreed comfortably that it was all very sad.

By the end of another day, they had confided in each other that the respective deaths were a merciful release. By another day, they had explained to each other—in bursts of confidence—that the deaths had released both of them from a type of hell. By the end of yet another day, they had both come to the conclusion that they were meant for each other.

"Those deaths were the hand of God," said Humphrey as he held Isabella in his arms under the blazing stars.

And by the time the happy couple found out that the deaths had been the hand of Sir Gerald Warby, they were well and truly married.

Alice was reconciled with her parents, who had traveled to London immediately after hearing about the attempt by Sir Gerald on the duke's life. Alice could hardly berate them for having driven off Sir Gerald and married her to a man with whom she was deeply in love. But the Laceys stayed with them in London until Alice began to wonder who was the mistress of the duke's establishment, herself or her mother. The duke, who had been treating Alice like glass, began to become tetchy, particularly after several evenings when he had gone to make love to his wife and found Mrs. Lacey sitting by Alice's bed reading to her.

The Laceys accompanied them to all social events, Mrs. Lacey saying frequently that it was not very fashionable for a duchess to look so, well, *doting* when she surveyed her husband.

At one ball, Mrs. Duggan took Alice aside and said, "I am off to Paris at the end of the week to join the colonel and I thought all was well with you. But your mama do go on running your life and Ferrant ain't looking too happy. And do remember that mothers can sometimes be jealous of daughters."

"What can I do?" asked Alice helplessly.

"What can a duchess do? A duchess can send her parents packing," said Mrs. Duggan.

"I must, I suppose," said Alice. "Oh, look! Mama is talking to Ferrant and goodness knows what she is saying, for he is looking like thunder."

Mrs. Lacey did not know she was jealous of her daughter. Such a thought would never have entered her mind. Her background of merchant class, however, often made her sensitive to what she saw as not enough respect in servants, and she was piqued that her many commands to Alice's servants were then taken to Alice herself, for her blessing, before any orders were carried out. She had just been telling the duke to be on his guard against Dunfear and Donnelly, particularly Donnelly. "For you know how silly Alice can be," she said, with an indulgent smile. "Did not Mr. Lacey and I try to save her from Sir Gerald?"

The duke, who had hitherto looked on Mr. Donnelly and Lord Dunfear as friends and saviors, began to think that young Donnelly paid just too much attention to his wife, and, what was more,

Donnelly had all the lethal charm of the Irish—and he was nearer Alice's age than the duke was himself. The jealousy that he swore would never plague him again engulfed the duke in a great green wave.

The trouble started in earnest on the following day when Alice learned that Mr. Donnelly and Lord Dunfear had called and had been told she was not at home when, in fact, she was dressed and waiting to go driving with them.

"His Grace's instructions," said Hoskins sadly.

Alice took a deep breath. She remembered her mother talking to the duke and how the duke's face had darkened. She now knew her mother very well—and knew instinctively that Mrs. Lacey had probably poisoned the duke's mind against Donnelly and Dunfear.

"Send Mr. Shadwell to me," she said coldly.

When the secretary came in, Alice said sharply, "As you are so good at arranging things, Mr. Shadwell, I wish you to tell my parents that their stay with me is at an end. You will then instruct the maids to pack their belongings and have the traveling carriage brought round. That will be all. I am going out shopping, and when I return, I want them gone."

A flicker of a smile crossed the secretary's face. "Very good, Your Grace. But if Your Grace would be kind enough to write these instructions for me, that would be a great help. Mrs. Lacey will not believe me, else."

Alice made an impatient noise and wrote down a terse set of instructions and handed them to him. Then, accompanied by Betty and a footman, she went off to look at the gewgaws at Exeter Exchange. She was being driven back by a groom in a light open carriage when she saw Mr. Donnelly and called to the groom to stop.

"Now what have I done wrong?" Donnelly said, smiling up at her.

"I fear my mother may have been warning Ferrant against you," said Alice, with a sigh. "Mama is leaving today. I confess her visit has been a great strain."

"Tell you what," said Mr. Donnelly, jingling change in his pockets, "had a lucky win at cards. Treat you to an ice at Gunter's."

"Good," said Alice. "That will give Mama more time to pack and leave."

The duke was strolling across Berkeley Square, feeling more at peace with the world and himself than he had felt for some time. Had he not vowed that he would never be plagued by this dreadful jealousy again? How on earth could he believe anything bad of those two Irishmen who had been instrumental in saving his life?

And then his eye fell on the window of Gunter's—and there was Alice, in a brand-new bonnet he had not seen before, laughing and talking to . . . Donnelly!

His first blind impulse was to run in and confront the pair. Common sense took over. There had been scandals enough. He could not bring himself to join them and talk to them civilly. The fact that it could hardly be an assignation—as Alice's maid, one of his own footmen, and a groom were waiting in the carriage outside—did nothing to damp his temper.

On his return home, even the news that his wife had sent her parents packing did not cheer him. He paced the drawing room, watched by the cynical eye of Oracle, reinstated in a large gilt cage.

The duke tortured himself with pictures of Alice in Donnelly's arms, the pair of them entwined in a passionate embrace. Alice *was* passionate. Alice did not behave like a lady. Had not Alice, dressed as Columbine, paraded the streets of London *showing her ankles*?

Alice arrived home. She learned the glad news that her parents had left and that her husband was waiting for her in the drawing room.

She tripped into the drawing room, swinging that new and frivolous bonnet by the strings—that bonnet that she had not worn for *him*.

Alice took one look at her husband's furious face and stood still. "What is the matter, dear?" she asked.

"What is the matter? You ask me what is the matter? You have the gall to parade about the streets of London—in a new bonnet—on the arm of that penniless Irish mountebank!"

"If you saw us, why did you not join us?" asked Alice.

"I could not *trust* myself to join you. What exactly is going on between you and Donnelly?"

"Nothing," said Alice, suddenly as angry as he. "May I remind you he saved your life."

"So what am I supposed to do?" he jeered. "Wrap you up in a parcel and hand you to him, saying, 'Take my wife with my grateful compliments'?"

"Now you are being silly," snapped Alice.

"How dare you address me in such a manner, madam!"

"I shall address you any way I like if it will bring you to your senses, although I am seriously beginning to doubt if you have any . . . senses, I mean."

He looked at her levelly. "This marriage was a mistake."

Alice gasped with hurt.

"Mr. and Mrs. Vere," announced Hoskins.

The duke and the duchess pinned social smiles on their faces. "Lucy," cried Alice, "you are looking so well."

Edward beamed with pride. "That's what a happy marriage does."

"I wouldn't know," said the duke evenly.

"Neither would I," put in Alice, not to be outdone.

Lucy and Edward exchanged anguished looks. "May I offer you some wine, Edward?" asked the duke sweetly. "My father-in-law presented me with a case of claret."

"Are your parents still here?" asked Lucy.

"They finally left," said the duke sourly before Alice could speak, "after having stayed about a century."

"Don't exaggerate," said Alice.

"It felt like a century."

Edward, who had been about to lower his bottom into a chair, stood up again. "My stars!" he said. "I quite forgot we were to call on Mrs. Duggan to say good-bye."

"Oh, yes," said Lucy eagerly. "Dear Mrs. Duggan."

"Let's hope she takes *dear* Mr. Donnelly with her when she goes," said the duke.

"You are stupid and childish," said Alice after they had left. Angry tears stood out in her eyes. "I will never speak to you again."

"Good!"

They faced each other like enemies, neither one wanting to be the first to quit the field of battle.

"You," said Oracle suddenly, "are a pair of twat-faced scullions."

"What did you say?" shouted the duke.

"Scullions. Twats," said Oracle. "Not a brain between you."

The duke stared at Alice and a sudden smile lit up his eyes. "What have you been saying to that bird?"

"It was not I. It must have been Sam, the groom, at Clarendon. He took care of Oracle when I was away. Oracle has learned the language of the stables."

"And the wisdom of the ages," said the duke softly. "He said we had not a brain between us."

He held out his hands. "Come to me, Alice. Come here to me and say you forgive me."

She flew into his arms.

"It was my mother, was it not, John?"

"Yes, and I was a fool to listen to her. Kiss me, Alice."

An hour later, she lay naked in his arms and murmured, "We were supposed to go to the opera tonight."

He kissed her breast.

"So we were."

"Much pleasanter here."

"Mmm."

"And we will never, ever quarrel again."

"Alice, my love, I swear it."

Three months later, Mrs. Duggan sat in her apartment in Paris and read a letter from Mr. Donnelly. "I am sure you are anxious for news of our duchess," he had written.

I was attending a breakfast at Lord Rother's—you know, where Doggie's wife met her end. The house is wonderfully refurbished, the merry widow having got Rother to open the purse strings wide. Lady Macdonald, back from Paris—in a gown bordering on the indecent—was there, and what must she do but flirt with Ferrant. Our little duchess picked up a jug of water and threw it full into Lady Macdonald's face. Ferrant takes his duchess to task for her behavior, and, in front of everyone, his wife slaps him. "That marriage is over for sure," says Lady Rother. I became anxious after all we had gone through for that couple and went in search of them.

There they were, in a quiet part of the gardens, kissing and hugging each other in broad daylight ... and in such a passionate way that it made this young Irishman blush, I can tell you ...

"Now that's what I call a happy marriage," said Mrs. Duggan, and began to laugh.

Romance at Its Best
from
Regency